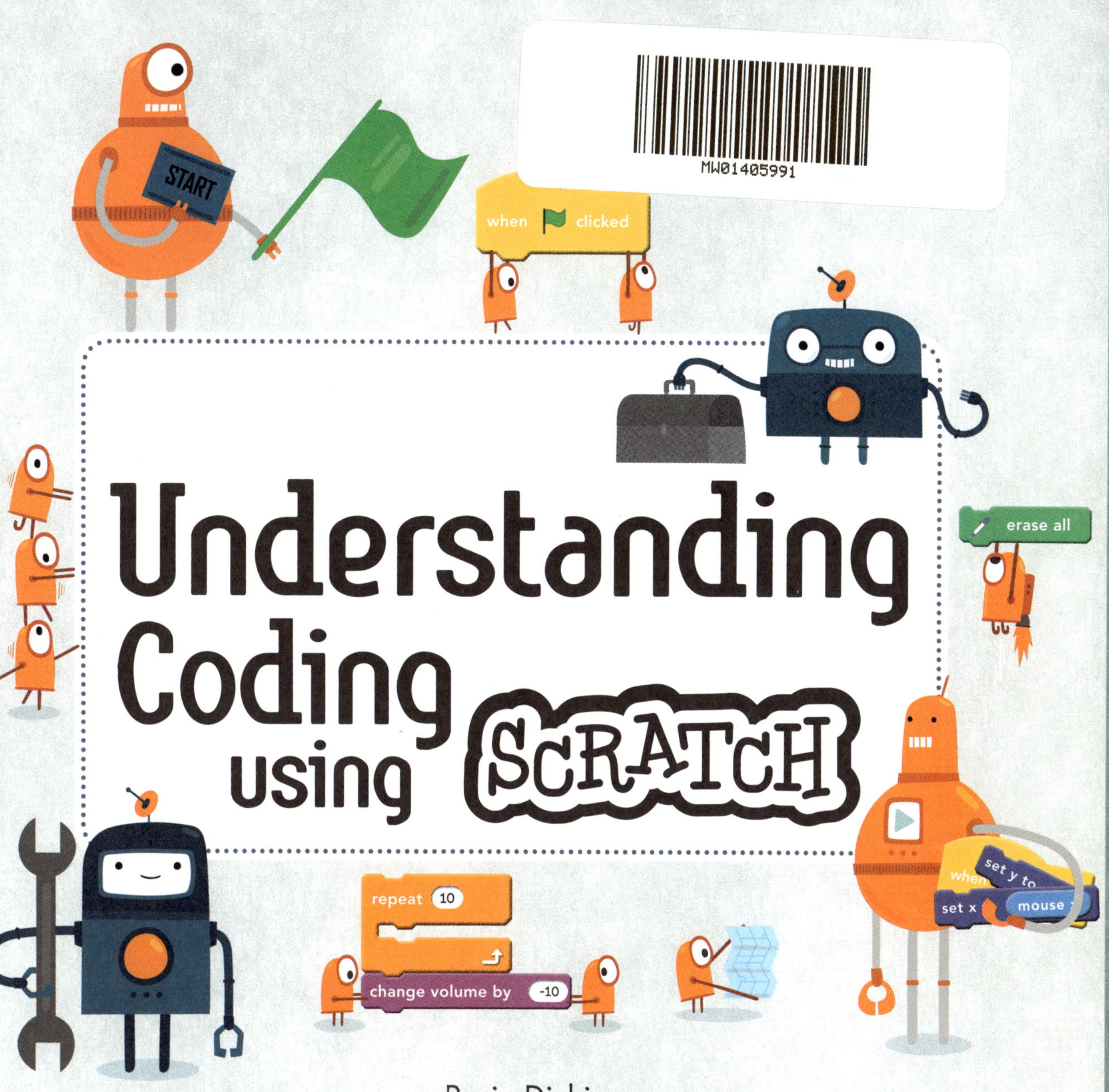

Understanding Coding using SCRATCH

Rosie Dickins,
Jonathan Melmoth & Louie Stowell

Coding consultants:
Berbank Green & Jonathan Skuse
Additional coding advice: Ben Woodhall

Illustrated by Shaw Nielsen
Designed by Stephen Moncrieff,
Matt Preston & Hayley Wells

Contents

when clicked

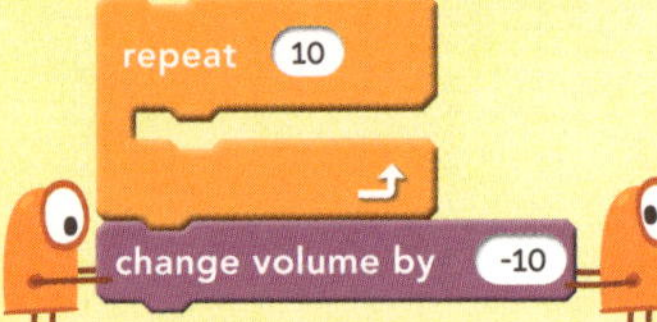
repeat 10
change volume by -10

say Hello! for 2 secs
go to front
wait 1 secs

stamp
rest for 0.25 beats
stop all

erase all
pen down
wait until

hide
stop all sounds
next costume

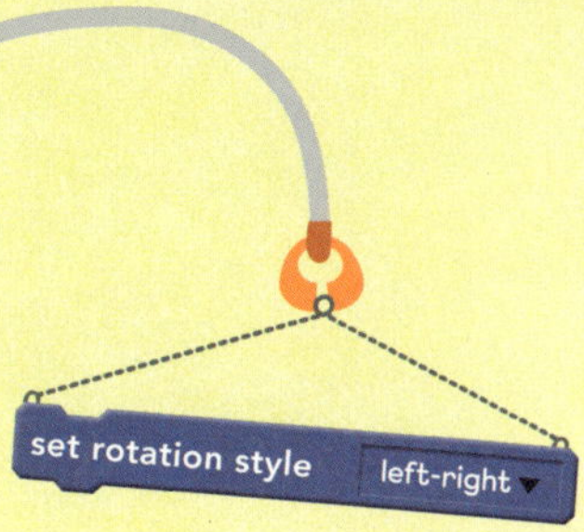

Games

Useful stuff

What is coding?

Coding means writing instructions for computers. A finished set of instructions is known as a program. If you learn to code, you can create programs of your own.

Being understood

For a program to work, it must be written in a way that the computer understands. That means breaking down all the instructions into clear, simple steps, and putting them into computer language.

WARNING!
Computers follow instructions blindly – they can't think for themselves. So everything must be spelled out clearly, leaving nothing out.

Computer language

Computer language is like ordinary language, but with a limited word list and precise rules about how to set things out.

There are many different computer languages, designed for different kinds of coding. The first one most people learn is called *Scratch* – a language made especially for beginners.

Scratch is great for making games and animations – and for learning about coding in general.

Scratch is developed by the Lifelong Kindergarten Group at the MIT Media Lab. See http://scratch.mit.edu

Why choose Scratch?

Scratch was designed to be quick and easy to use. It allows you to build up programs by slotting together ready-made blocks of code.

Look out for boxes like this one. The green boxes explain KEY IDEAS. Blue boxes have TIPS on using SCRATCH.

About this book

This book will show you how to make the most of Scratch by creating animations, stories and games – along with lots of tips for writing your own code. All the examples are broken down into short, easy-to-follow steps.

Getting started

The simplest way to use Scratch is on the Scratch website. All you need is a computer and an internet connection.

Go to **usborne.com/Quicklinks** and type in the name of this book, for a link to the Scratch website and full instructions, as well as other useful coding resources. You will also find a link to finished, working code for all the programs in this book.

Please follow the online safety guidelines at Usborne Quicklinks.

If you want to use Scratch offline (without being connected to the internet), you can download the language and save it onto your computer. Just follow the instructions at **Usborne Quicklinks.**

Starting Scratch

When you start up Scratch on your computer, you will see this screen.

On the Scratch website, click 'Create' (in the purple bar) to get here.

The **green flag** and **red button** are used as start and stop buttons.

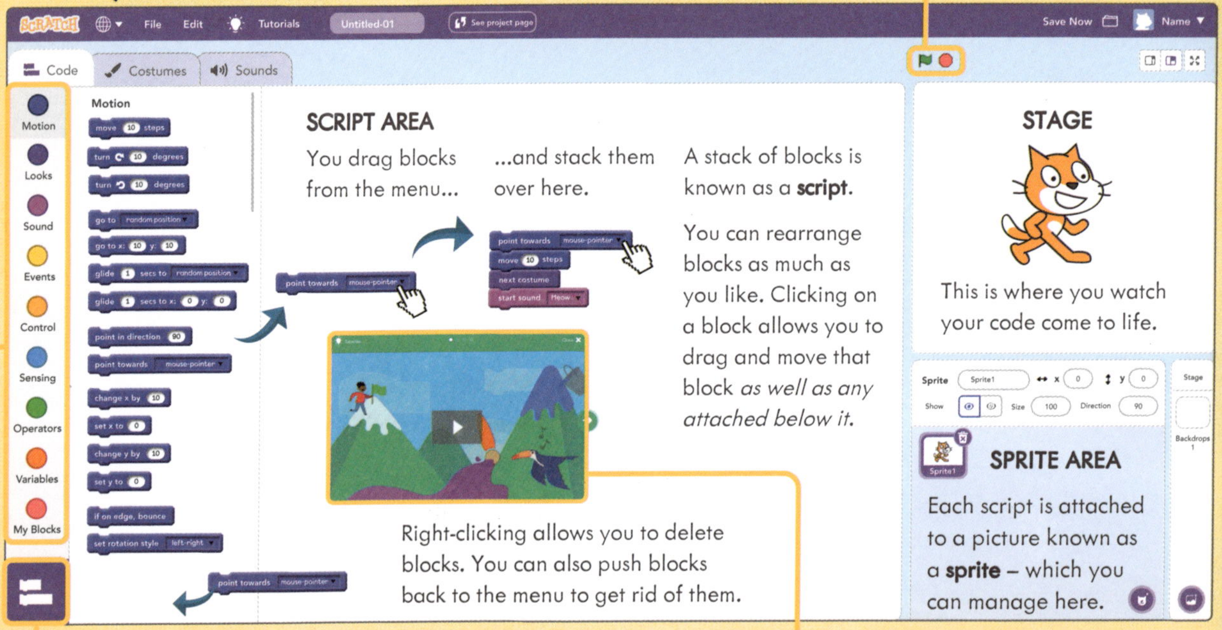

SCRIPT AREA

You drag blocks from the menu...

...and stack them over here.

A stack of blocks is known as a **script**.

You can rearrange blocks as much as you like. Clicking on a block allows you to drag and move that block *as well as any attached below it.*

STAGE

This is where you watch your code come to life.

SPRITE AREA

Each script is attached to a picture known as a **sprite** – which you can manage here.

Right-clicking allows you to delete blocks. You can also push blocks back to the menu to get rid of them.

These names are the **block menus** – see below for how they work.

This button opens **Extensions** which gives you access to **music** and **pen blocks.**

You may have to close a tutorial box before you start. Click on the small 'x' to close it.

Block menus

Each **block menu** contains a variety of different, color-coded blocks. For example...

- **Motion** menu blocks (blue) make sprites move.
- **Looks** menu blocks (purple) change how things look.
- **Control** menu blocks (orange) control the scripts themselves.

Click on a **block menu** name to bring up the blocks available, or turn to page 82 for a full list.

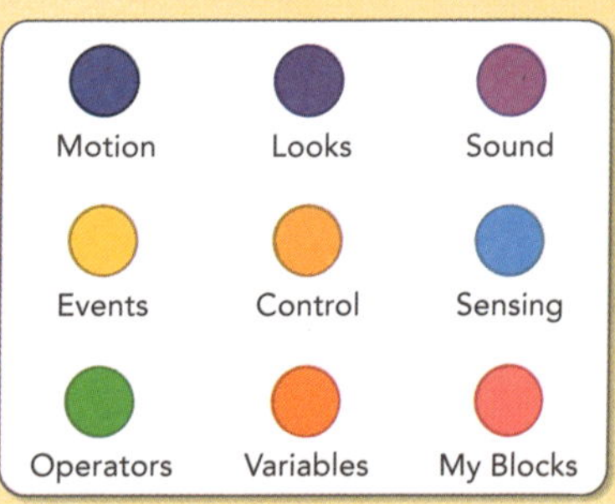

These are the nine **block menus.**

First steps

1 Try dragging these three blocks (from the **Motion menu**) into the **script area** to make the cat walk...

Then click on the **Sound** menu and add a **start sound** block.

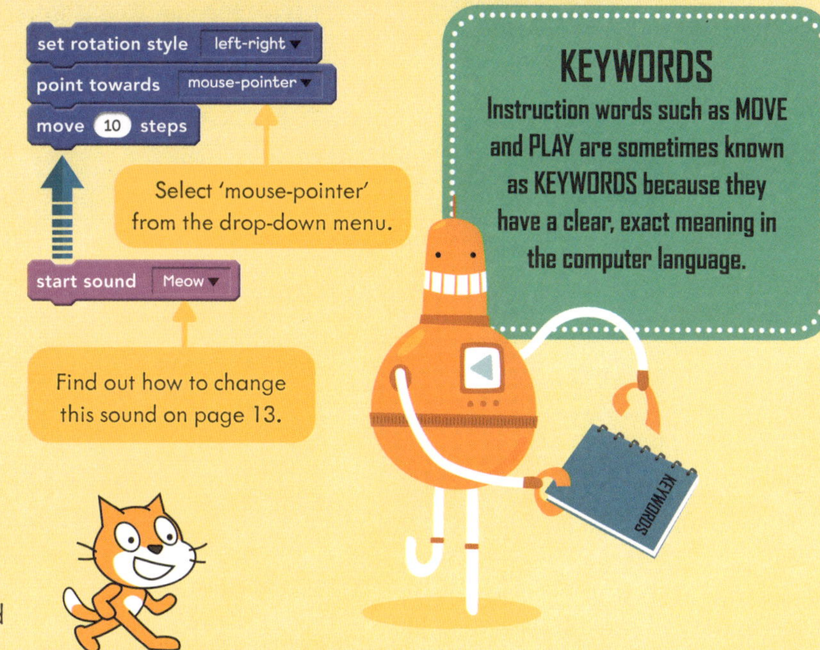

KEYWORDS

Instruction words such as MOVE and PLAY are sometimes known as KEYWORDS because they have a clear, exact meaning in the computer language.

2 Click on the script to **run** it. Click a few times and watch what happens.

The script glows as it runs, and the cat moves and meows. (If the cat goes too far, you can drag it back again.)

Congratulations, you've written your first piece of code!

3 But the cat doesn't look as if it's walking. For that, its feet need to move...

Click on the **Looks** menu and add a **next costume** block. This changes to another picture or 'costume' of the same sprite (in this case, the cat with its feet in a new position). Click on this script a few times.

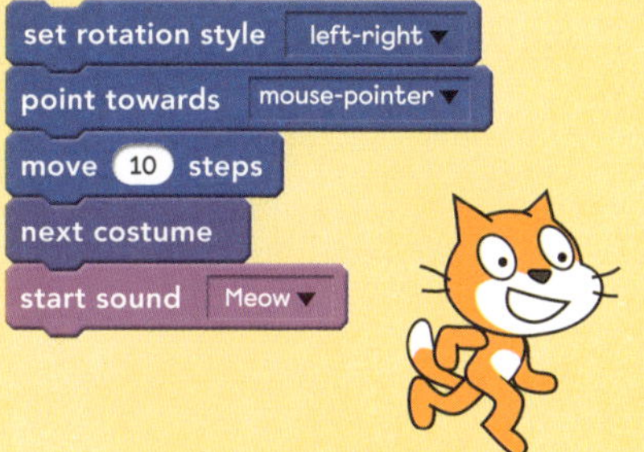

4 The cat's feet move – but only when you click on the script. To keep things going, you need to go to the **Control** menu for a **repeat** block. This block makes all the instructions inside it repeat, or **loop**, as many times as you tell it.

You can type into the little white boxes to change the numbers.

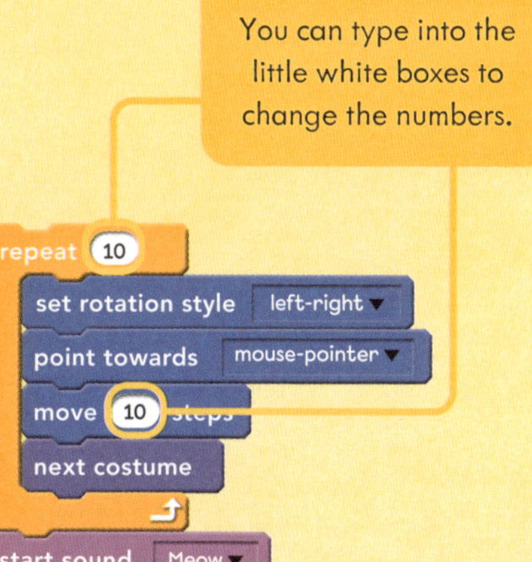

LOOPS

LOOPS are used a lot in all kinds of code, because they make programs much shorter and quicker to write.

Turn the page to see how to turn this script into a simple cat-and-mouse game.

Cat and mouse

The object of this game is to keep your mouse-pointer one step ahead of the cat. If the cat touches the mouse-pointer, it says, "Got you!" and the game is over.

1 This game requires a new kind of loop: **repeat until** (from the **Control** menu)...

...plus a diamond-ended block from the **Sensing** menu.

2 Snap them together (the loop will expand to fit). Then click on the black triangle and select 'mouse-pointer' from the drop-down menu.

3 Go back to the script from the last page. Click on the first block in the loop, then drag that block, along with all the blocks attached below it, into your new loop.

4 Finish with a **say** block (from the **Looks** menu).

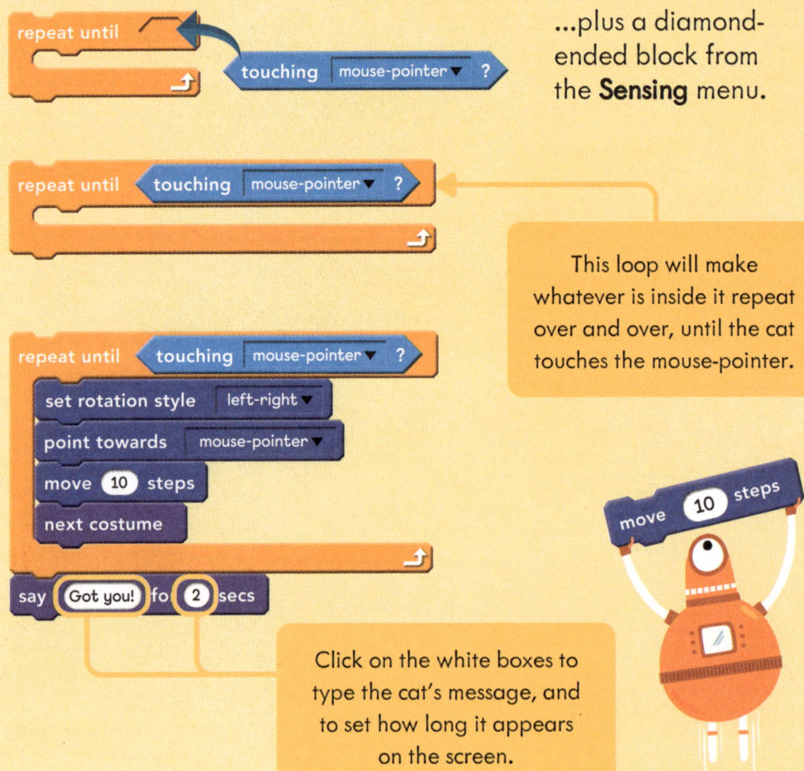

This loop will make whatever is inside it repeat over and over, until the cat touches the mouse-pointer.

Click on the white boxes to type the cat's message, and to set how long it appears on the screen.

Testing your script

5 Click on the script and move your mouse-pointer around. The cat should follow your mouse until it catches you. Try it a few times.

If the cat hits the edge of the **stage**, it flickers. But you can fix this by inserting a **bounce** (from the **Motion** menu) at the start of the loop...

CONDITIONALS

Instructions such as IF and REPEAT UNTIL tell the computer to react differently to different conditions (in this case, where the cat is). So they are known as CONDITIONAL instructions.

IF your code works, give yourself a pat on the back.

Notice how the blocks are shaped so they only fit together in certain ways...

6 You can also make the script easier to use by adding a **green flag** block (from the **Events** menu) at the start.

Now you can run the script by clicking on the **green flag** above the **stage.** (Or click on the **red button** to stop it.)

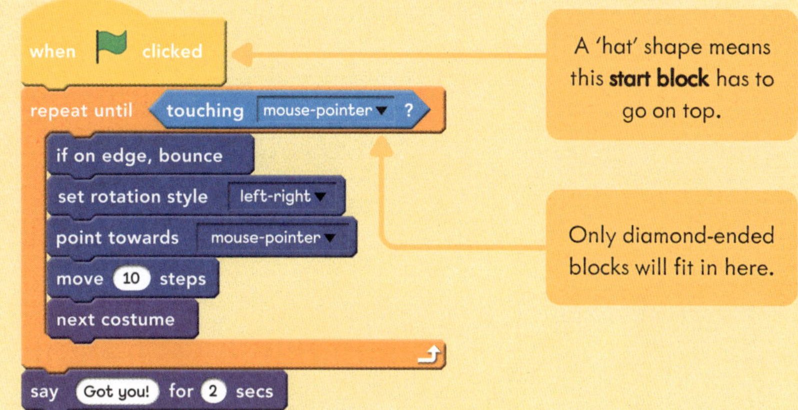

SYNTAX

The way you set out your code is known as SYNTAX. If the syntax is wrong, the computer will get muddled. Luckily, you can't go wrong in Scratch. The blocks will only snap together if the syntax is correct.

So I'm always right!

7 To make the game fairer, you can make the cat start in the middle of the **stage** each time. Add a **go to x y** block (from the **Motion** menu).

Then you can set the position with coordinates...

```
when [green flag] clicked
go to x: (0) y: (0)
repeat until <touching [mouse-pointer] ?>
    if on edge, bounce
    set rotation style [left-right]
    point towards [mouse-pointer]
    move (10) steps
    next costume
say [Got you!] for (2) secs
```

If you want the cat to start in the middle, type '0' in both boxes.

COORDINATES

You can define any point on the stage as amount 'x' across and 'y' up-down. These x and y amounts (or values) are known as COORDINATES.

When x and y are zero, you're in the middle.

Keeping score

On these pages, you can find out how to improve your cat-and-mouse game by keeping score, and add a cartoon mouse using an extra sprite.

Vital variables

As you play the game, your score will change. So to help the computer keep track of it, you need to give this piece of information (or 'data') a name. In coding, this is known as **making a variable...**

VARIABLES

A variable is like a named STORAGE BOX. You can change the contents as often as you like, but still refer to it by the same name. You can pick any name you like, the computer won't mind – for example,

'Score' 'High score' 'Fred'

Making a variable

1 Go to the **Variables** menu (one of the **block menus**) and click on 'Make a Variable'. Type 'score' into the box that pops up (you can leave the button pressed 'For all sprites'). Then click 'OK' and...

...you will get a set of new 'score' blocks.

Leave the box at the top checked to make the variable display on the **stage** (the part of the screen where your code comes to life).

2 Insert a **set score** block at the start. (Drag it over the right spot, and it will snap into place when you let go.)

Insert a **change score** block into the loop, to add a point each time you dodge the cat.

Try the game now. You should see a score counter in the corner of the **stage**, with the score going up and up until you are caught.

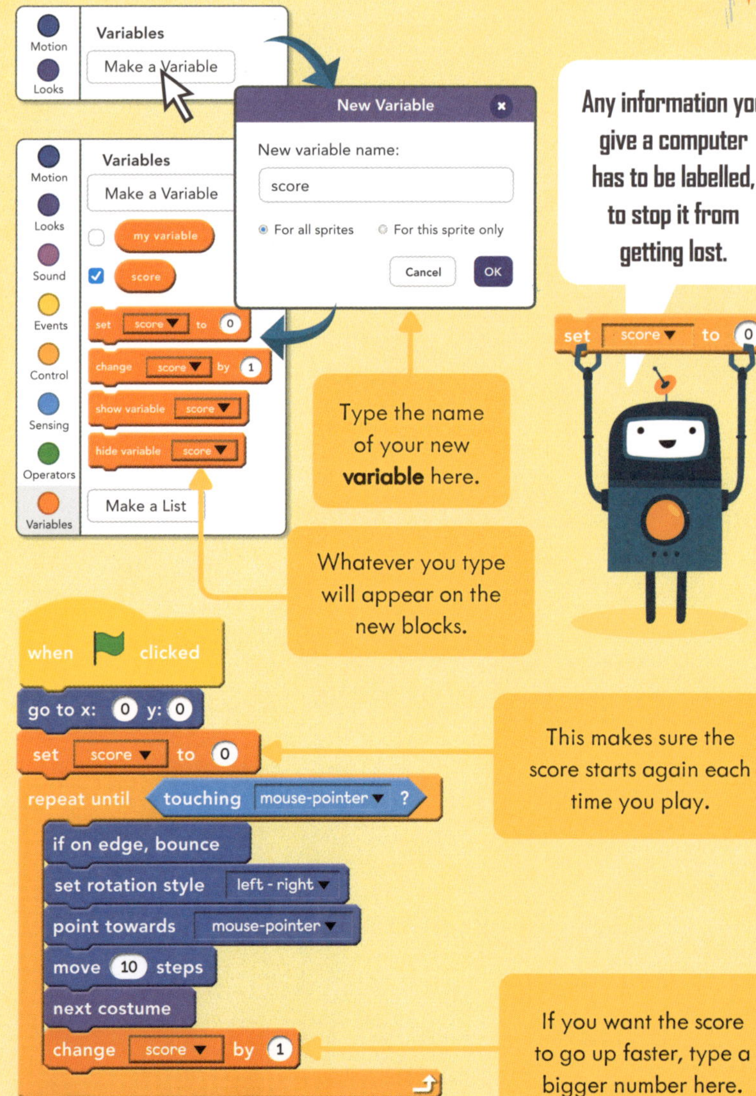

Adding another sprite

Now let's add a cartoon mouse for your cat to chase.

1 Find the little picture of a cat at the bottom of the **sprite area**. Click on it to bring up the **Sprite Library**. Scroll through to find 'Mouse1'.

2 Click on 'Mouse1'. It will appear on the **stage** with the cat...

...and in the **sprite area**. (The **script area** will be empty, because you haven't written anything for the mouse yet.)

3 Create a new script to control the mouse. Use a **go to x y** block to make the mouse start in the same place each time.

Use a **repeat until** loop, with a **touching** block (from **Sensing**), to make the mouse keep moving until it's caught.

4 Select the **cat sprite** and change 'mouse-pointer' to 'Mouse1' both times it appears. The cat will now chase the new mouse sprite, which in turn follows your mouse-pointer.

5 Click the **green flag** to start the game. This starts all the scripts at the same time.

Play the game a few times and see how high a score you can get.

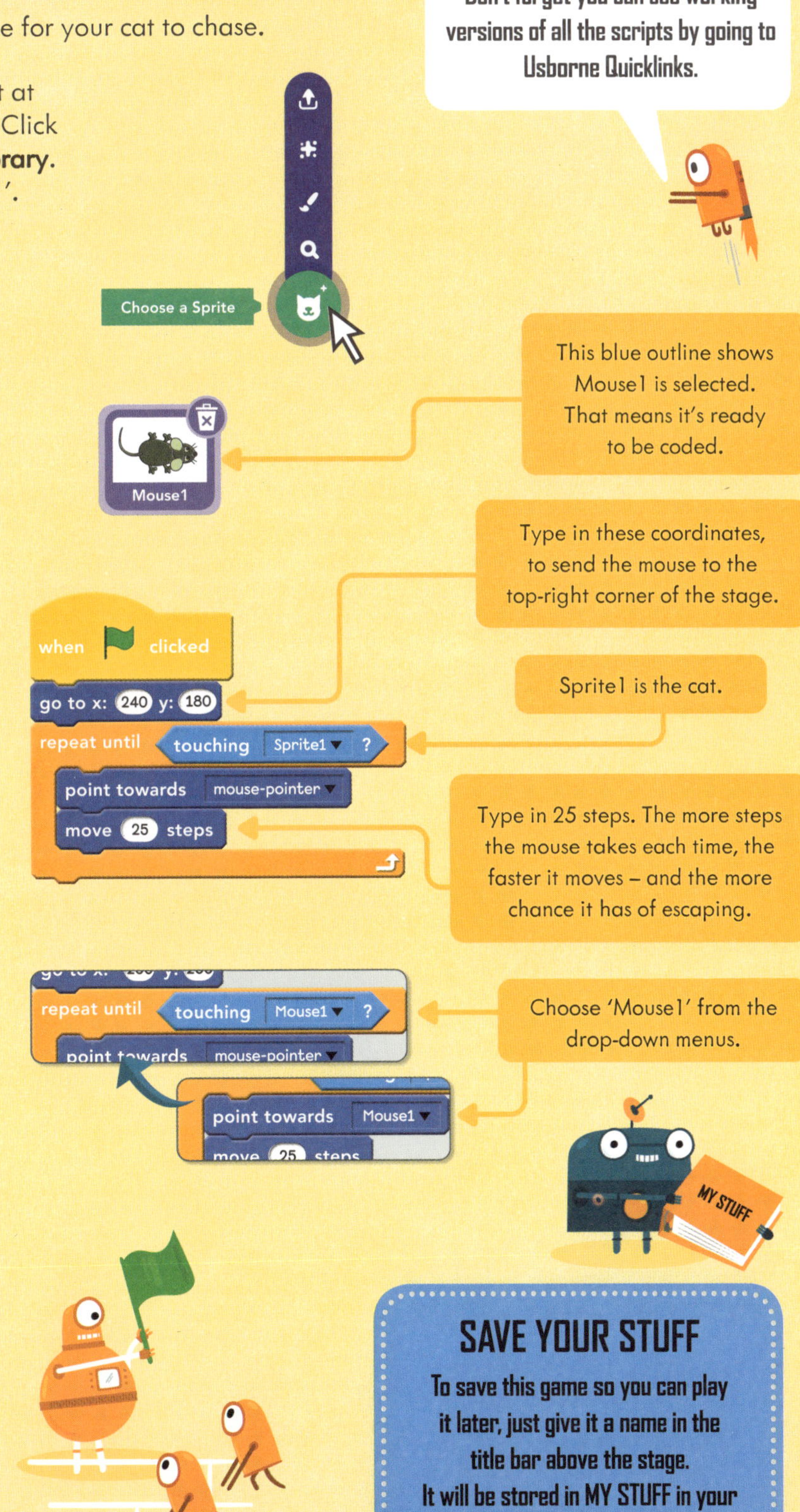
Don't forget you can see working versions of all the scripts by going to Usborne Quicklinks.
Choose a Sprite
Mouse1
This blue outline shows Mouse1 is selected. That means it's ready to be coded.
Type in these coordinates, to send the mouse to the top-right corner of the stage.
when clicked
go to x: 240 y: 180
Sprite1 is the cat.
repeat until touching Sprite1 ?
point towards mouse-pointer
move 25 steps
Type in 25 steps. The more steps the mouse takes each time, the faster it moves – and the more chance it has of escaping.
repeat until touching Mouse1 ?
point towards mouse-pointer
Choose 'Mouse1' from the drop-down menus.
point towards Mouse1
MY STUFF

SAVE YOUR STUFF

To save this game so you can play it later, just give it a name in the title bar above the stage. It will be stored in MY STUFF in your Scratch account (see page 80).

Dancing sprites

Use **costumes** to animate a sprite, and set its moves to music.

Different versions of the same sprite are called **costumes.** You can view all of a sprite's available costumes by clicking the **Costumes** tab (above the **block menus**).

Most sprites come with a few costumes. You can also create new ones – find out how on page 29.

Bring a dinosaur to life

1 Start a new project by clicking on 'File – New' (in the purple bar). Click on the trash can to delete the cat and clear the stage.

Sprite1

Choose a Sprite

2 Click on the **sprite** button at the bottom of the **sprite area** to bring up the **Sprite Library.** Click on a sprite to select it – we chose 'dinosaur4'.

1	2	3	4
dinosaur4-a 120 x 146	dinosaur4-b 150 x 145	dinosaur4-c 120 x 146	dinosaur4-d 145 x 181

The dinosaur has 4 costumes altogether.

3 Create this script to make the dinosaur keep changing costume. Click on the green flag above the stage to run it.

```
when [green flag] clicked
forever
    next costume
    wait (0.5) secs
    move (10) steps
    if on edge, bounce
```

If you insert a small pause here, it will give you time to see each costume before it changes.

The dinosaur starts to move. But if it bounces off the edge, it flips upside down! To keep it on its feet, you need to set the **rotation style...**

ANIMATIONS

All animations work by stitching together still pictures like this. The more gradual the changes between pictures, the smoother the effect.

4 Insert a **set rotation style** block (from the **Motion** menu) at the start of the loop.

Select an option from the drop-down menu. Try them all and see what happens.

```
when [green flag] clicked
forever
    set rotation style [left-right ▼]
    next costume
    wait (0.5) secs
    move (10) steps
    if on edge, bounce
```

'left-right' – changes direction, but keeps the sprite upright.

'don't rotate' – keeps the sprite exactly the same.

'all around' – lets the sprite spin around.

Adding music

You can also add music for the dinosaur to dance to.

1 Click on the **Sounds** tab and then on the tiny picture of a speaker at the bottom of the page, to open the **Sound Library**.

2 Click on **Loops** and choose a tune. Click on it to select it. It will now appear in the list of sounds *and* as an option on some **Sound** blocks.

3 Go back to the **Code** tab and create another script, like this.

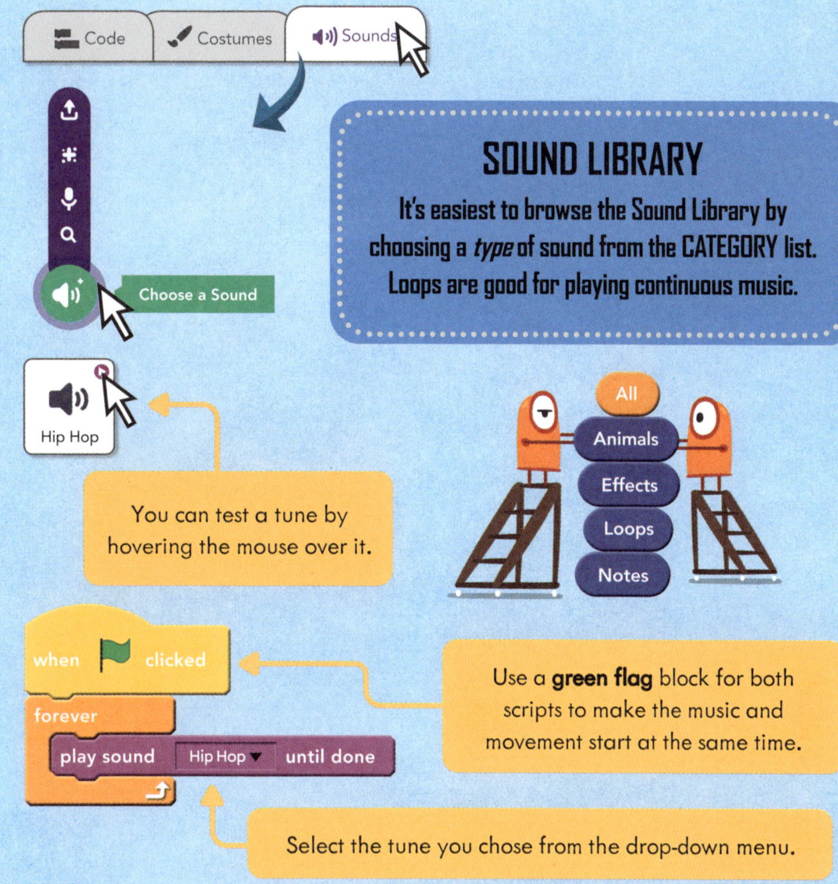

Setting the scene

Finally, add a **backdrop** to finish the animation.

1 Click on the little picture of a landscape at the bottom of the **sprite area**, to open the **Backdrop Library**. Scroll down until you find a backdrop you like.

2 Click on the backdrop to make it appear on the stage. Then click on the green flag to see the dinosaur dance in your chosen setting.

Build a band

Here, you can use **Music blocks** to assemble a band of sprites, then conduct them in a tune.

Setting a beat

1 Start a new project. Hide the cat by clicking on the **hide symbol** at the top of the sprite area.

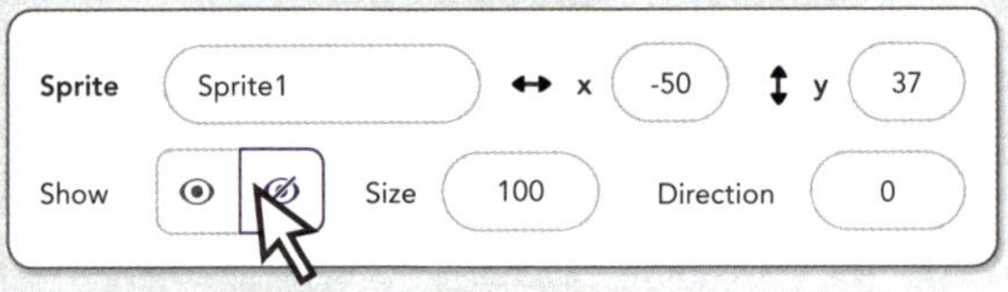

Sprite | Sprite1 | x -50 | y 37
Show | Size 100 | Direction 0

2 **Music blocks** are in **Extensions.** Click on the **Extensions** button at the bottom of the block menus to open **Extensions.**

Music
Play instruments and drums.

3 Select **Music.** This will make an extra menu of **Music blocks** appear.

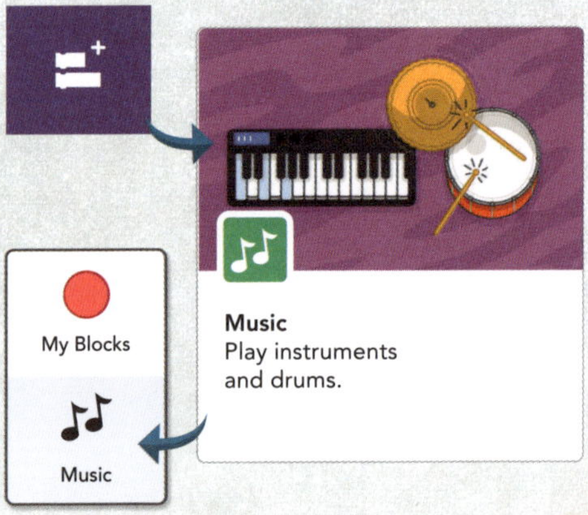

My Blocks
Music

4 Click on the **Music** menu and drag out a **drum** block.

Select which kind of drum, and how long it will play.

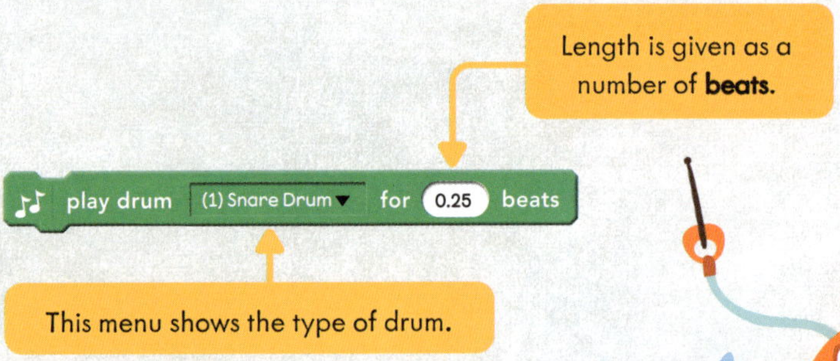

```
play drum (1) Snare Drum ▾ for 0.25 beats
```

Length is given as a number of **beats.**

This menu shows the type of drum.

5 Build up a short sequence like this. Then add a **forever** loop (from **Control**) and **green flag** block (from **Events**), so it will keep going once you click the flag.

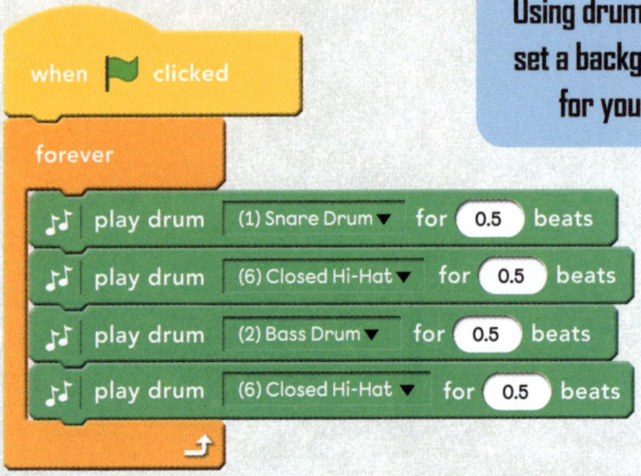

```
when ⚑ clicked
forever
    play drum (1) Snare Drum ▾ for 0.5 beats
    play drum (6) Closed Hi-Hat ▾ for 0.5 beats
    play drum (2) Bass Drum ▾ for 0.5 beats
    play drum (6) Closed Hi-Hat ▾ for 0.5 beats
```

Using drum blocks will set a background beat for your band.

Adding instruments

You can add more sprites to play more instruments.

1 Choose a new sprite to be your musician.

2 Give it a **set instrument** block and pick an instrument from the drop-down menu.

3 Instruments need to be combined with **note** blocks to make a sound. This controls which note will play, and for how long.

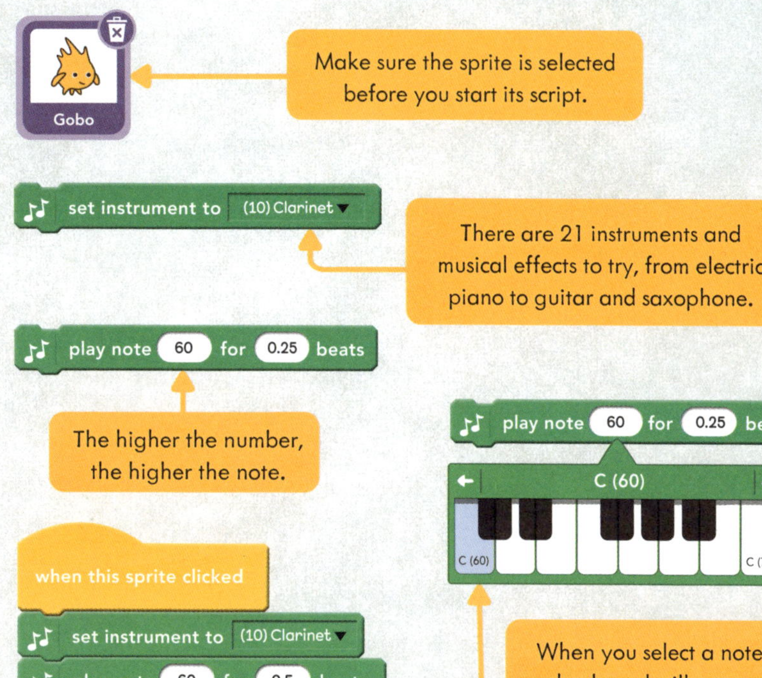

4 Add a **when this sprite clicked** start block. This will make the instrument play when you click the sprite on the stage.

To create and play a tune, add more **note** blocks to make a sequence.

when this sprite clicked
set instrument to (10) Clarinet
play note 60 for 0.5 beats
play note 55 for 0.25 beats
play note 64 for 0.25 beats
play note 60 for 0.5 beats

When you select a note, a keyboard will appear and show you which note you are choosing.

Now try adding more sprites to complete your band...

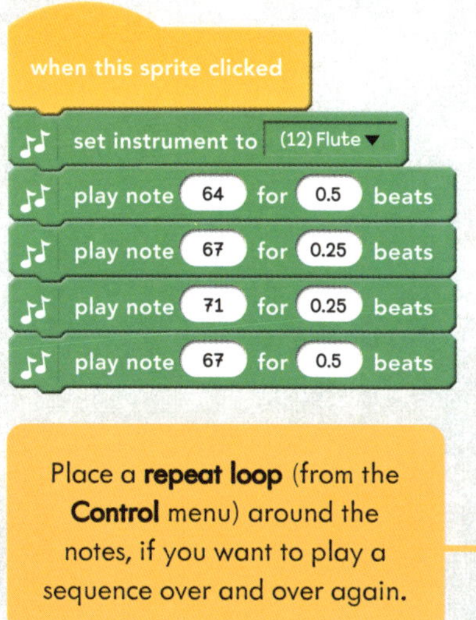

Place a **repeat loop** (from the **Control** menu) around the notes, if you want to play a sequence over and over again.

More sounds

You can add different sound effects and record your own sounds for your band of sprites.

Using sound effects

1 Create a new sprite. Then, select the **Sounds** tab at the top of the **script area.**

2 Click on the **speaker** button to bring up the **Sound Library.**

3 Choose a sound and hover the mouse over it to hear it. Keep browsing until you find a sound you like, then click to select it.

4 To make the sound play when you click the sprite, go back to the **Code** tab. Then create this script with a **start sound** block (from the **Sound** menu).

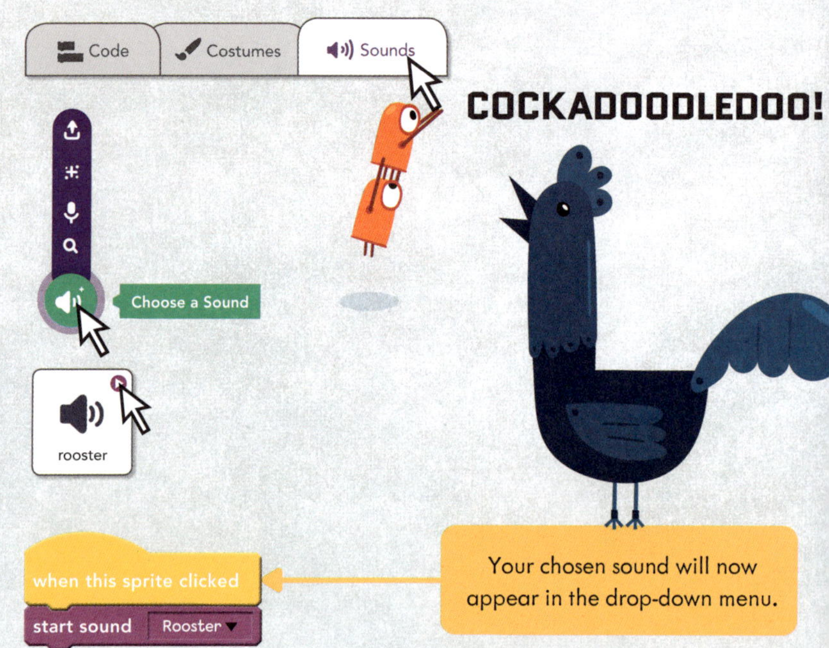

Recording your own sounds

1 Select the **Sounds** tab and hover the mouse over the speaker button. A new set of buttons will pop up.

2 Click on the **microphone** and a **Record button** will appear. Click **Record** and make the sound you want. Click **Stop** when you're done.

3 Now when you use a **start sound** block, your recording will appear in the drop-down menu.

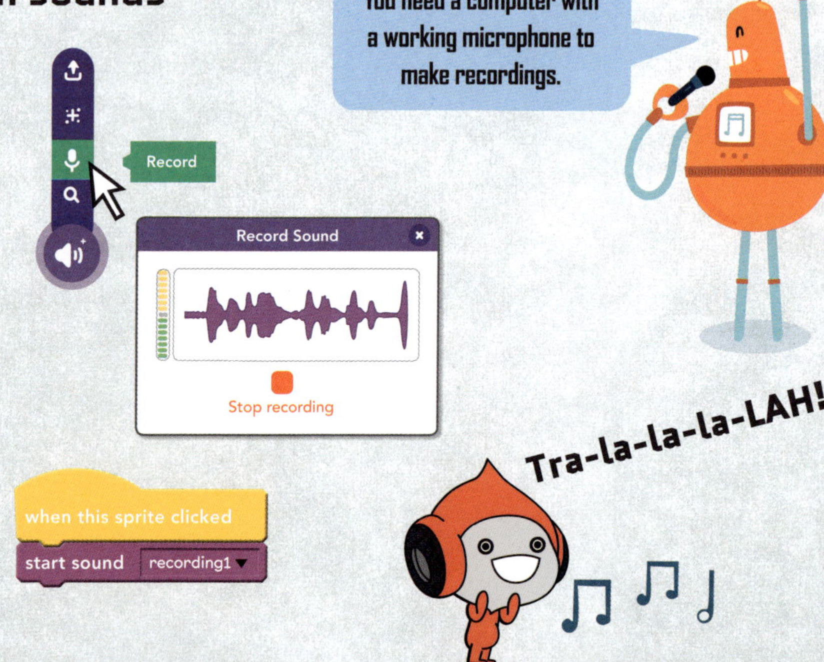

Faster and slower

The speed of music is called the tempo. You can set it faster or slower, and even change it while your band plays.

Setting the tempo

1 To set the tempo for a particular sprite, go to the **music** menu and add this block to the start of its script.

set tempo to 120
The higher the number, the faster the music.

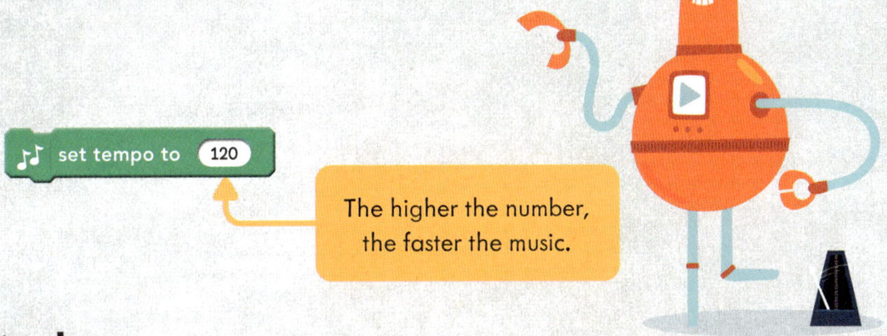

Creating speed controls

1 Create two arrow sprites to use as controls – one for making the tempo faster, the other for slowing it down – and arrange them on stage. For each, click on the arrow and then 'Direction', in the **sprite area**. Use the spinner to make it point up or down.

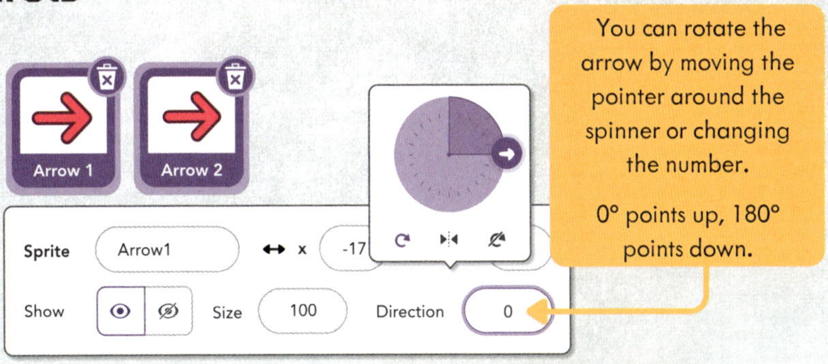

Arrow 1
Arrow 2
Sprite
Arrow1
x
-17
Show
Size
100
Direction
0
You can rotate the arrow by moving the pointer around the spinner or changing the number.
0° points up, 180° points down.

2 Open the **Sound Library** again and click on 'pop'. Then select the 'go-faster' sprite in the **sprite area** and create this script.

when this sprite clicked
start sound Pop
change tempo by 10
Adding a 'pop' noise makes it clearer when you click.
This increases the speed by 10.

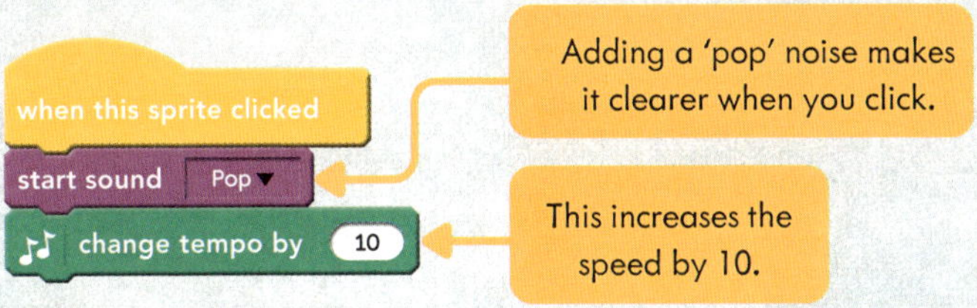

3 Select the 'go-slower' sprite in the **sprite area** and create this script for it.

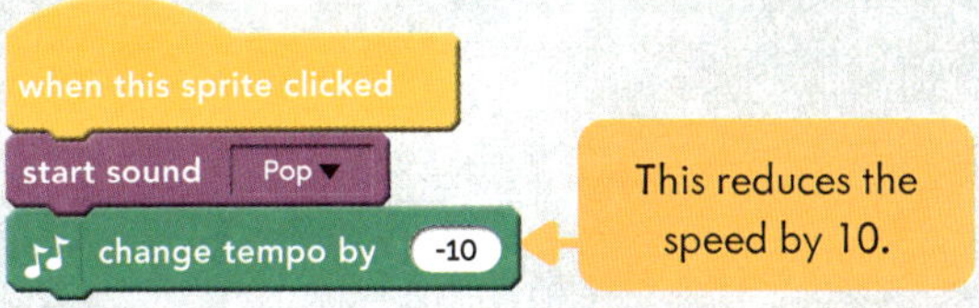

when this sprite clicked
start sound Pop
change tempo by -10
This reduces the speed by 10.

4 Try clicking the controls while your band is playing. Do you like the sound? If not, play around with your code a bit more.

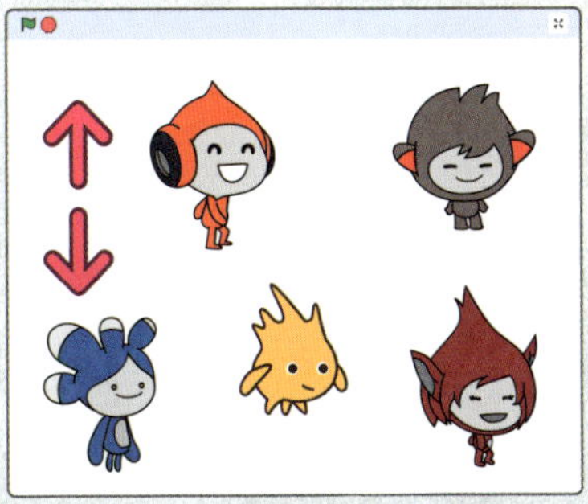

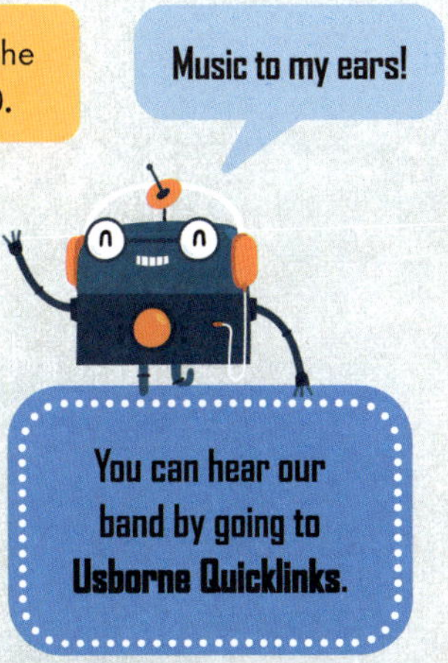

Music to my ears!
You can hear our band by going to Usborne Quicklinks.

Boo!

Discover how you can make a sprite look ghostly, appear and disappear, and sneak up on the unwary.

Make a ghostly sprite

1 Start a new project, and click on the trash can to delete the cat. Open the **Sprite Library** and choose a spooky sprite, or go to **Usborne Quicklinks** (see right) for an Usborne sprite.

Usborne Quicklinks has lots of sprites and other stuff you can use. Just go to **usborne.com/Quicklinks** and type in the name of this book.

2 Take a **green flag** block (from the **Events** menu). Then, add a **go to x y** block (from **Motion**). Set x and y to zero.

Now it's time to make it look ghostly...

This sends the sprite to the middle of the screen.

Ghost effect

3 Go to the **Looks** menu, take a **set effect** block and add it below. Choose 'ghost' from the drop-down menu. This will make the sprite look faint and ghostly.

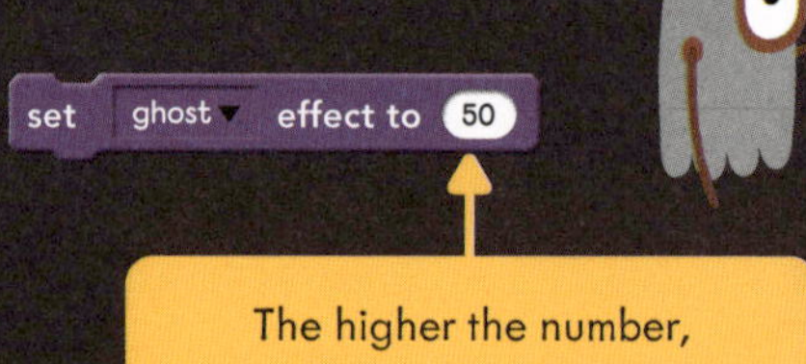

The higher the number, the stronger the effect, up to 100% (completely invisible).

4 Take a **repeat loop** (from **Control**) and wrap it around a **change effect** block (from **Looks**). Select 'ghost' from the drop-down menu again. Add the loop to the end of your script.

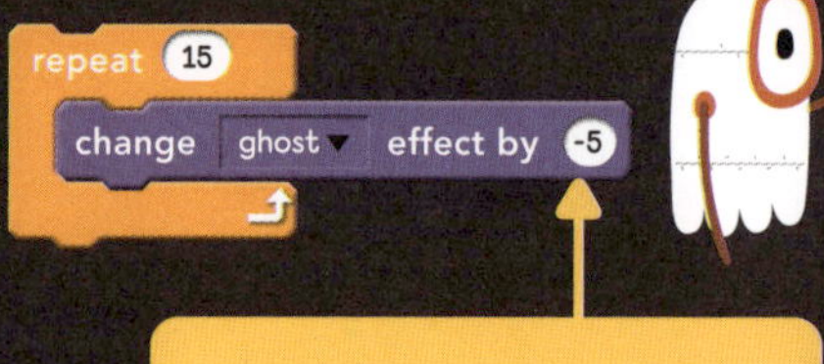

A minus number will reduce the effect – so the sprite slowly becomes more solid.

SPECIAL EFFECTS

Scratch has several different effects you can choose from. Here are a few of them...

WHIRL makes a sprite swirl around.

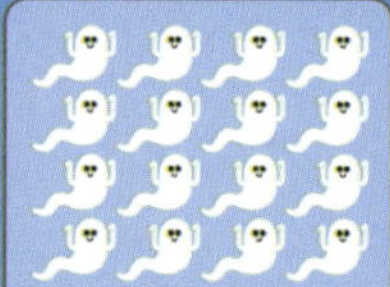

MOSAIC creates lots of little copies.

FISHEYE makes a sprite swell in the middle.

5 For a spooky sound effect, go to the **Sounds** tab. Click on the **speaker** button, select a sound and click 'OK'. Then add a **start sound** block (from the **Sound** menu).

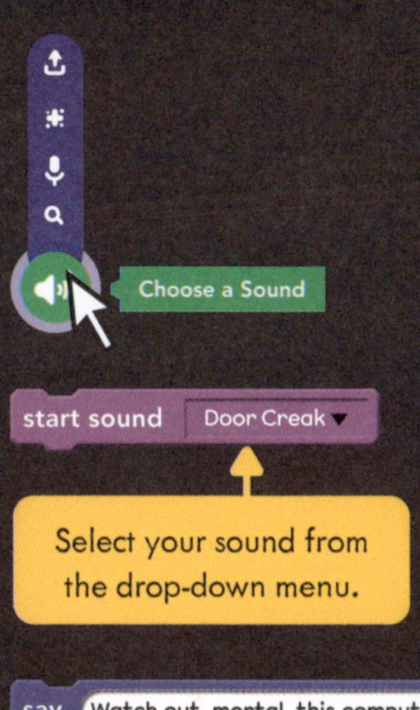

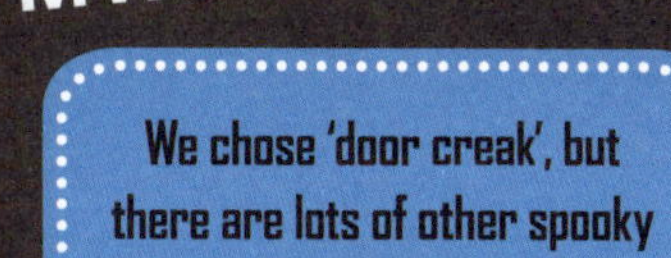

We chose 'door creak', but there are lots of other spooky sounds to try...

scream1
scream2
screech
crazy laugh
wolf howl

6 You could add a **think** or **say** block (from **Looks**) to add some dialogue, too.

Your code so far should look something like this... Run it and tweak anything you're not happy with.

```
when [flag] clicked
go to x: 0 y: 0
set ghost effect to 50
repeat 15
    change ghost effect by -5
start sound Door Creak
say Watch out, mortal, this computer is haunted! for 3 secs
```

You could add a spooky backdrop, too. (See page 13 for a reminder of how.)

On the move

7 To make the ghost move smoothly, take a **glide** block (from the **Motion** menu). Add it to the bottom of your script.

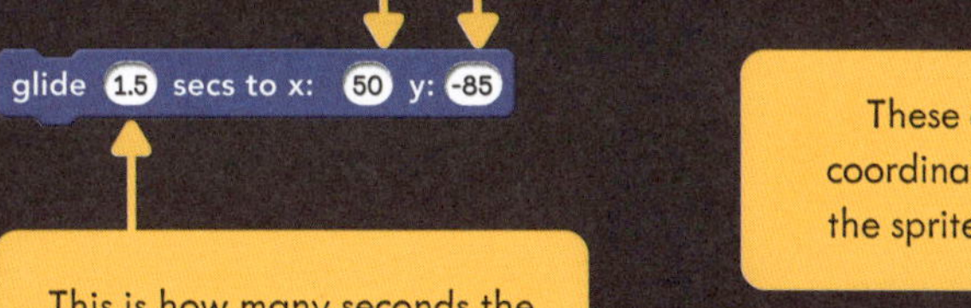

These are the coordinates where the sprite will stop.

This is how many seconds the glide will take. The bigger the number, the slower the glide.

8 To make the sprite seem to get closer, add a **change size** block (from **Looks**) to the bottom of your script.

The bigger this number, the bigger the sprite gets. (A minus number will shrink it.) When the sprite gets bigger, it seems closer.

9 You could add more **think** or **say** blocks underneath the **change size** block, to continue the story.

```
change size by (100)
say (Wooooooooo!) for (3) secs
```

Hide and seek

10 To make the sprite disappear, add a **hide** block (from **Looks**).

Then add a **wait** block (from **Control**) to make everything pause.

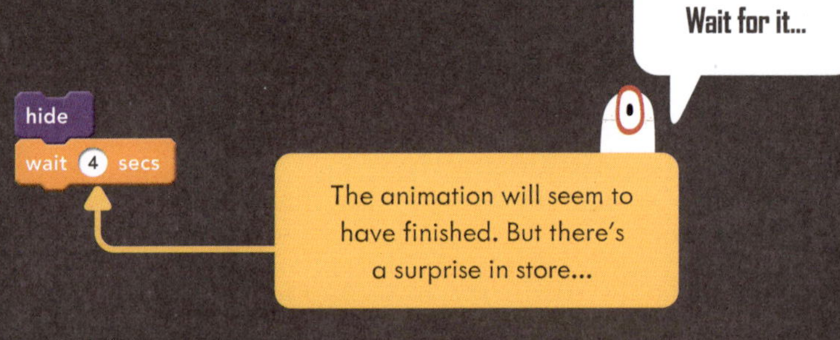

Surprise!

11 Add a **go to** block (from **Motion**), to send the sprite to a new spot. Then, go to the **Looks** menu and add a **show** block to reveal it, and a **change size** block to make it suddenly bigger.

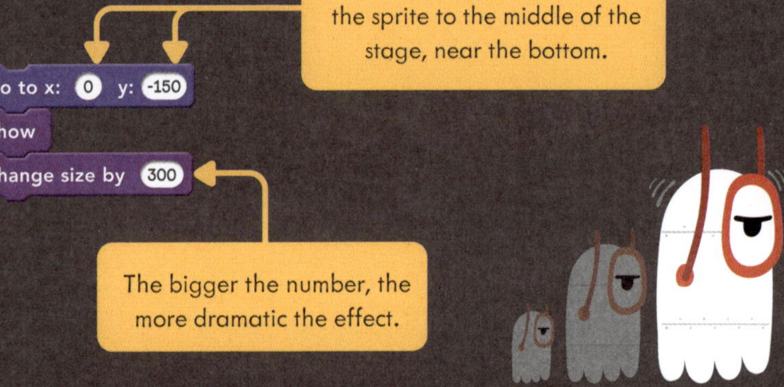

12 You could also add a surprising sound effect with **start sound**, then make the sprite say something like 'BOO!' with another **say** block and a **wait** block to pause for effect.

13 You could finish by making the sprite disappear (with another **hide** block), or add some more dialogue...

Testing

14 Click on the green flag to run your animation. Try it a few times.

If you run it more than once, the sprite will start at the wrong size. To fix this, you need to insert a **set size** block (from **Looks**) at the start.

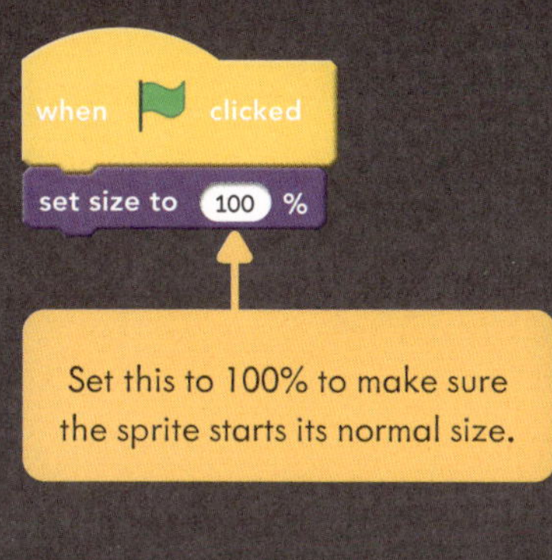

In Scratch, if you want your animation or game to start the same way each time, you need code at the start of your script to CANCEL OUT any instructions you give by the end.

The finished code

This is the finished code for our version – which you can play by going to **Usborne Quicklinks.**

The whole animation is a single script.

Drawing

Here, you can find out how to turn your sprite into a pen, and use loops to make it draw different shapes.

1 **Pen** blocks are in **Extensions.** Click on the **Extensions** button at the bottom of the block menus. Then select **Pen** to see the menu of **Pen** blocks.

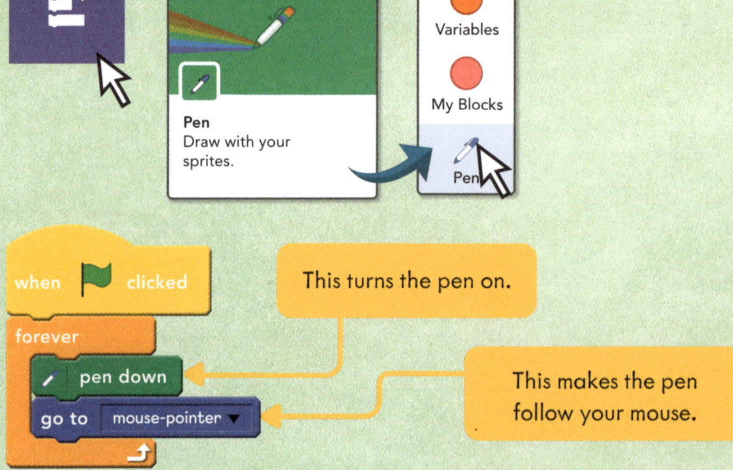

2 To draw using the mouse, start a new project and slot together these blocks.

3 Then click the green flag, and move your mouse around the stage.

The sprite acts as your pen, leaving a trail as it moves around the stage.

USEFUL PEN BLOCKS

This turns the pen OFF. — pen up

This makes the pen thicker or thinner. — set pen size to 3

Size 1
Size 5
Size 10

The bigger the number, the thicker the line.

This sets the pen to a particular color.

First click inside the circle... — set pen color to ...then click anywhere in the Scratch window to choose a color.

This changes the color. — change pen color by 10

In Scratch, each color has a number. Changing the number changes the color, and repeated changes create a rainbow effect.

Making shapes

You can also draw geometric shapes.

1 Delete the script from the previous page. Start a new script with these blocks, to clear the stage and position your sprite before you begin.

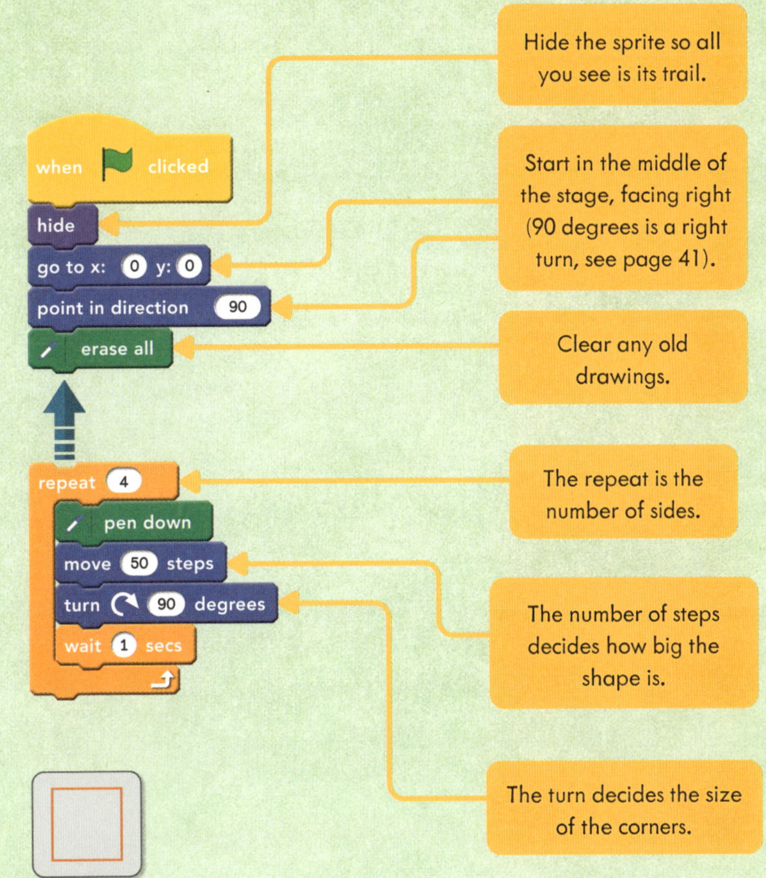

2 With these blocks you can draw many different kinds of shape (see below).

Adding a **wait** block makes the sprite pause after drawing each line, so you can see what's happening.

A **repeat** of 4 and a **turn** of 90 makes a square.

To make different shapes, all you need to do is change the numbers in the loop.

JOINING UP
As long as your repeat and turn multiply to make 360, the shape will join up (a full turn is 360 degrees).
360°

Shape patterns

To draw a shape again and again, so it makes a pattern, you can remove the **wait** block and add an extra loop, like this.

You can add a **change color** block for a multicolored effect.

Change the line thickness with the **set pen size** block.

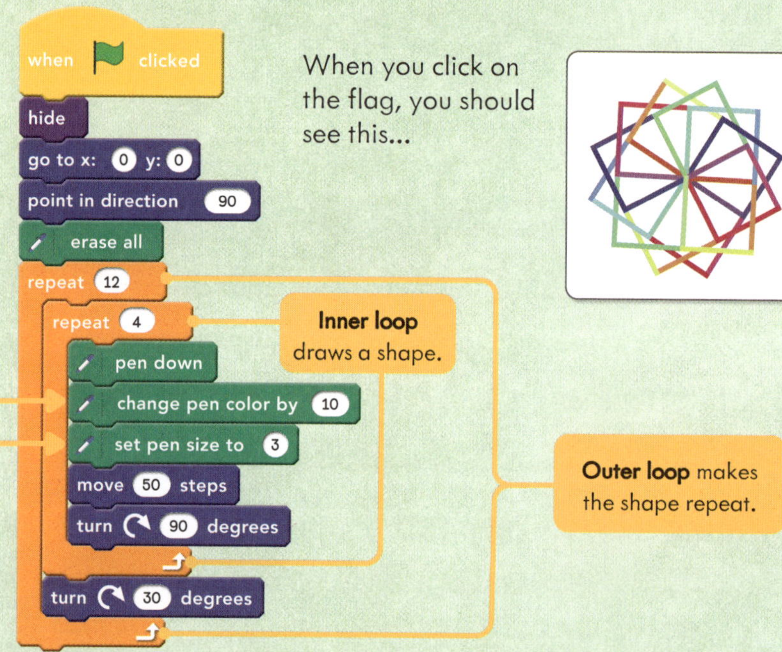

When you click on the flag, you should see this...

Changing the numbers of repeats and turns can create very different patterns. Experiment and see what you get.

If the outer repeat and turn values multiply to make 360, the pattern will go all the way around. (360 degrees is a circle.)

1 Outer loop: **repeat** 10, **turn** 36
Inner loop: **repeat** 3, **turn** 120

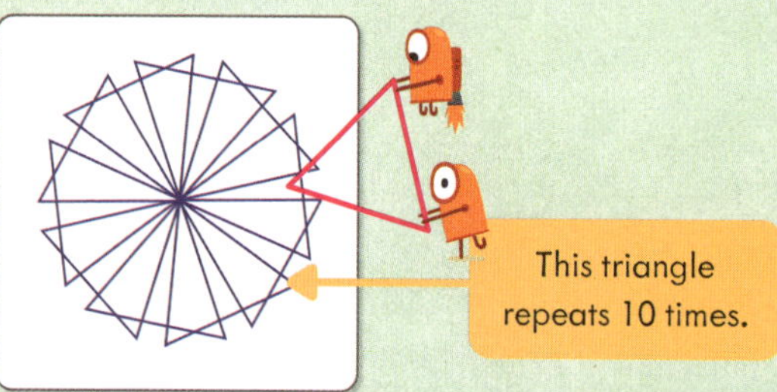

This triangle repeats 10 times.

2 Outer loop: **repeat** 45, **turn** 8
Inner loop: **repeat** 3, **turn** 120

3 Outer loop: **repeat** 12, **turn** 30
Inner loop: **repeat** 10, **turn** 36

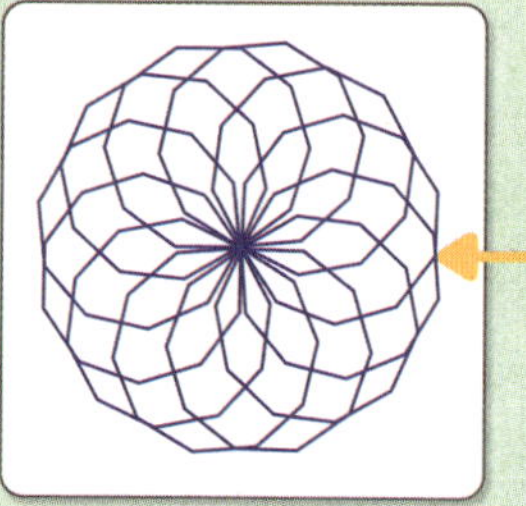

Replace **change pen color** with **set pen color** to draw in a single color.

Shape sliders

You can use variables to create slider controls, to make changing the shapes quicker and easier.

1 Go to **Variables** and select 'Make a Variable' (keep 'For all sprites' selected). Create two new variables: **shapes** and **sides.** Make sure the boxes next to the new variables are checked, so they appear on the stage.

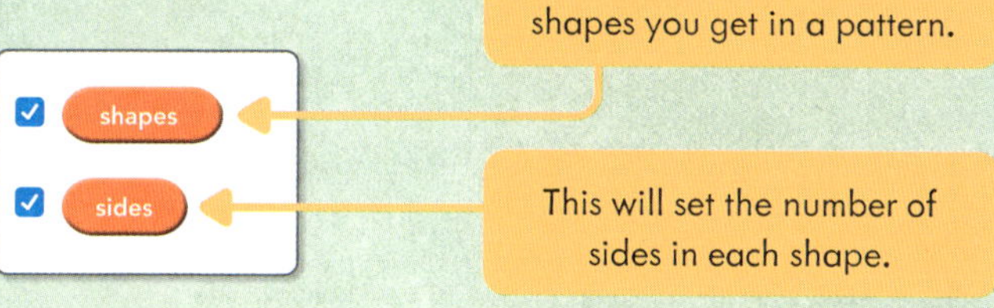

shapes
sides
This will decide how many shapes you get in a pattern.
This will set the number of sides in each shape.

2 Replace the value in the *outer* **repeat** loop with a **shapes** variable, and the one in the *inner* **repeat** loop with a **sides** variable.

3 In the **turn** blocks, replace the values with **divide** blocks from the **Operators** menu (see page 36). In coding, / is used as a 'divide' sign (÷).

Make the *inner* **turn** 360 / **sides.** Make the *outer* **turn** 360 / **shapes.**

If your shapes get too big, reduce the number of steps.

This makes sure each shape joins up.

This makes the shapes repeat all the way around.

4 Now to turn your variables into sliders. On the **stage,** right-click on **shapes** and select 'slider'. Right-click again to 'change slider range'. This makes the slider easier to use. Then do the same for **sides.**

Now you can play around with patterns by moving the sliders and clicking the green flag, instead of changing your code.

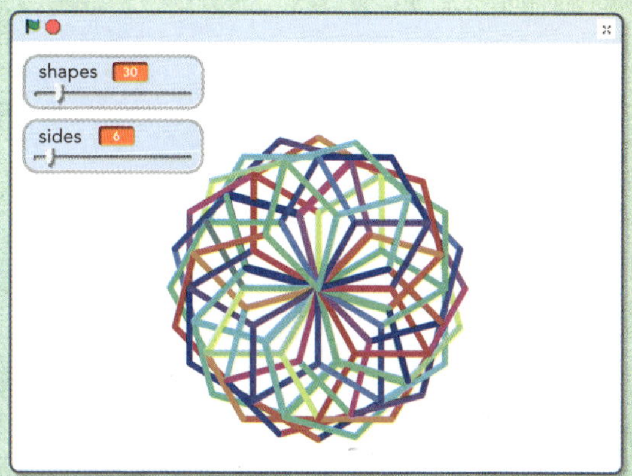

For the sliders, set shapes to 1-100, and sides to 3-20 (you can't have a shape with fewer than 3 sides).

Once upon a time

Find out how to use Scratch to make up animated stories, with backdrops, dialogue and surprise twists.

Choosing characters

1 Start a new project and delete the cat. Then click on the **sprite** button to open the **Sprite Library**. Select two characters by clicking. These sprites will now appear on the stage.

Adding a backdrop

2 Look for the **backdrop** button at the bottom of the **sprite area**. Click on it to open the **Backdrop Library**.

3 Scroll until you find a backdrop that you like, then click to select it. This is where your story will start.

Drag the characters to arrange them against the backdrop.

Can't see one you like? Find out how to use photos as backdrops on page 31, or paint your own on page 54.

Broadcasting a message

To get your story moving, you'll need a new type of block called a **broadcast** block. You'll find this in the **Events** menu.

BROADCASTING AND RECEIVING

In Scratch, BROADCAST blocks are used to send messages from one script to another. RECEIVE blocks listen out for a particular message. If the right message is received, it triggers a new script.

4 Select Pico (or whichever sprite will speak first). Give it a **green flag** block (from **Events**). Then add a **say** block (from **Looks**) and type its words into the white box.

This gives you time to read it.

5 Go to the **Events** menu and add a **broadcast** block. Click on the box and select 'new message', then type a name in the pop-up window.

We called the message Giga 1, because it's the first message sent TO Giga.

Receiving a message

6 Select the other sprite and give it a **receive** block. Add a **say** block and type in a reply, like this.

Choose the message the sprite is waiting for from the drop-down menu.

Testing your scripts

7 Click on the green flag to test the scripts so far. You should see Pico speak, followed by Giga replying.

MESSAGING

Most computer languages have a way of sending messages between different parts of a program. This is known as MESSAGING.

A longer conversation

8 You can keep broadcasting back and forth to create a whole conversation. Give each broadcast a different name, so they don't get mixed up.

First script for Giga

Each time you create a broadcast, it is added to this drop-down list.

Pico 1 is the first message being sent TO Pico.

PLANNING

To help you plan the conversation, you could write it out like this...

P: Hello Giga!
G: Hi Pico!
P: Let's go somewhere fun.
G: I have an idea.

This is especially useful as the SCRIPT AREA only displays the scripts for one sprite at a time.

Let's go somewhere fun.

Pico

Second script for Pico

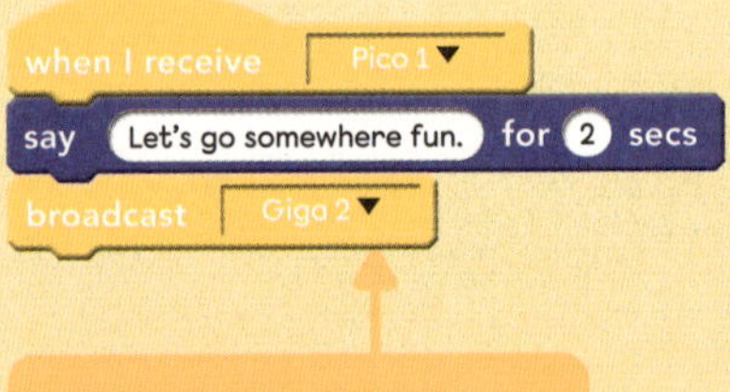

This is the second message being sent to Giga.

COPYING CODE

If you find you're using the same blocks again and again, you can right-click on a set of blocks and duplicate it.

Second script for Giga

This broadcast is going to trigger a surprise... you'll find out what below.

I have an idea.

Giga

A change of scene

9 To change the backdrop, click on the **backdrop** button at the bottom of the **sprite area**. Select a new backdrop. (We used 'moon'.)

It's like a scene change in a play.

Now tell the computer when to change the backdrop...

10 Click on the **stage** to the right of the **sprite area.** This will let you write a script for the stage.

11 Start a new script with **when I receive** and select 'Go to Moon' (Giga's last broadcast). Add a **switch backdrop** block (from **Looks**) and select 'moon'.

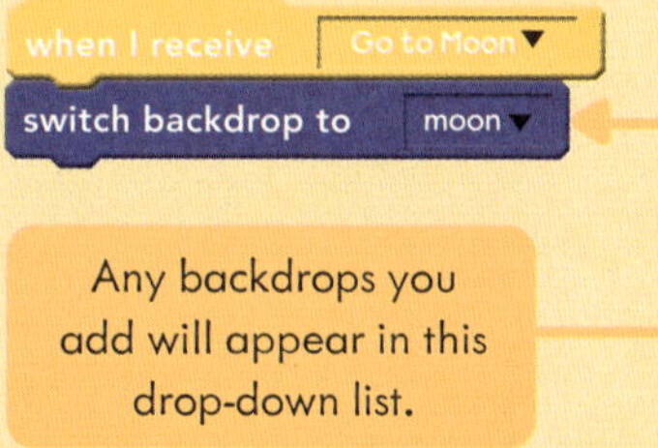

Any backdrops you add will appear in this drop-down list.

ATTACHING SCRIPTS

You can attach scripts to the STAGE or to the SPRITES you are using. (You can't attach scripts to a backdrop.)

Creating reactions

To make the sprites react to the change, you can create a new script triggered by the switch.

12 Select Pico, and start a new script with **when backdrop switches.**

13 So the pace doesn't feel rushed, add a 'wait' block. Then, add a **switch costume** block (from **Looks**) to make Pico look surprised.

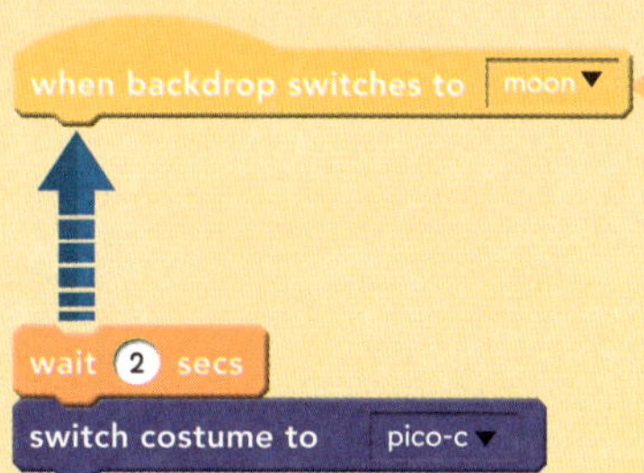

Select your new backdrop from the drop-down menu.

This is my surprised face.

CREATING COSTUMES

If you can't find the costume you want, you can use the PAINTING TOOLS (see page 32) to create a new one.

1. Right-click on a costume and duplicate it.

2. Then go to the COSTUMES tab and paint your changes on top.

It's easy to add details such as angry eyebrows.

Yes, I have one eye and two eyebrows. Deal with it.

Making an ending

14 You could add some more dialogue and costume changes to finish the story...

After typing in the words, add another **broadcast** block to make the other sprite respond.

This costume shows Giga with a mischievous smile.

Debugging

Click on the green flag to run the animation again. If you run it twice, you'll notice that it starts with the wrong costumes and background the second time.

DEBUGGING

Fixing problems, or BUGS, in code is known as DEBUGGING. Hardly anyone gets everything right first time, so debugging is an important skill to learn.

15 You can fix this by creating an extra script for each sprite, and for the stage, like this...

Add this script to Pico...

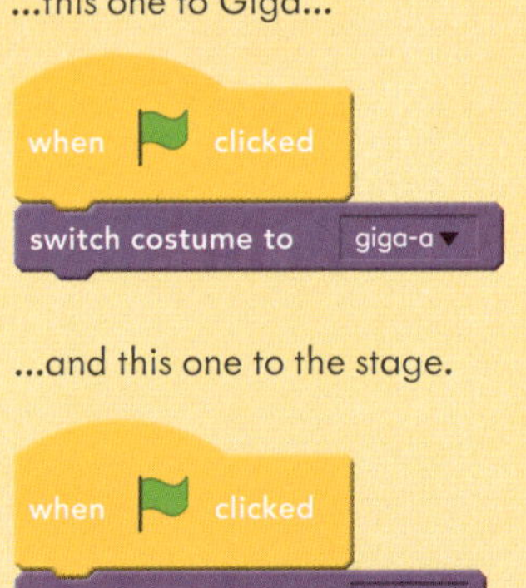

More ideas

You could add more elements to your story by using some of the code you learned earlier in this book. You could...

...add a soundtrack (see page 13)...

...add another sprite...

...or make your sprites grow, shrink or disappear (see page 19).

Uploading backdrops

You can also give your characters even more places to explore by uploading your own backdrops. You can take a digital photograph or find an image you like – but it must be a **.jpg** or **.png** file, no bigger than **10MB** in size.

1 To upload a backdrop, hover the mouse over the **backdrop** button, then select **Upload Backdrop** from the top of the list.

2 Find the file you want, click on it and press 'OK'. The new image will appear in the **Backdrops** tab.

FILE TYPES AND SIZES

The letters after the dot in a file name show what TYPE of file it is; .jpg and .png are both types of image file.

The size of files is measured in units known as BYTES or MEGABYTES (MB); 1MB is about a million bytes. The bigger a file, the more space it takes up in the computer's memory.

CROPPING

If your image isn't an exact fit, it will leave a border around the edge of the stage. You can fix this by trimming or CROPPING the image before you upload it, using an image-editing program such as Microsoft Paint, or a photo-editing program. (See **Usborne Quicklinks** for more advice.)

Painting sprites

You can create your own sprites using the **painting tools.** Here's how to do it.

Starting to paint

Start a new project and delete the cat. Hover the mouse over the **sprite** button, then select the **Paint** option to make the **painting tools** (see below) appear.

Select the tool you want by clicking on it. Then click in the **script area** to start painting.

Whatever you paint will appear in the script area (which becomes your painting area) AND on the stage.

Changing modes

Scratch has two painting modes...

Bitmap mode is good for painting freehand.

Vector mode makes it easier to create smooth lines and neat shapes.

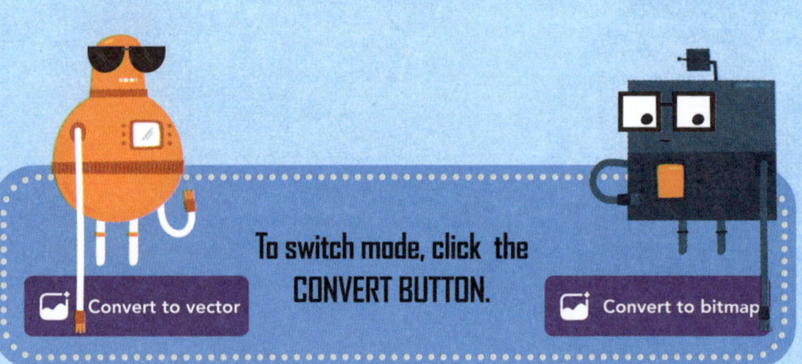

BITMAP TOOLS

- Make a line with the mouse
- Make a round shape
- Write text
- Erase
- Make a straight line
- Make a rectangle
- Fill an area with color
- Select an area

VECTOR TOOLS

- Select an object
- Make a line with the mouse
- Fill an area with color
- Make a straight line
- Make a rectangle
- Reshape an object (by dragging out points)
- Erase
- Write text
- Make a round shape

MORE VECTOR TOOLS

Extra tools appear when you start painting.

Forward	Forward a layer
Backward	Back a layer
Front	Top layer
Back	Bottom layer
Group	Group
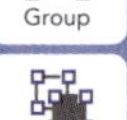 Ungroup	Ungroup

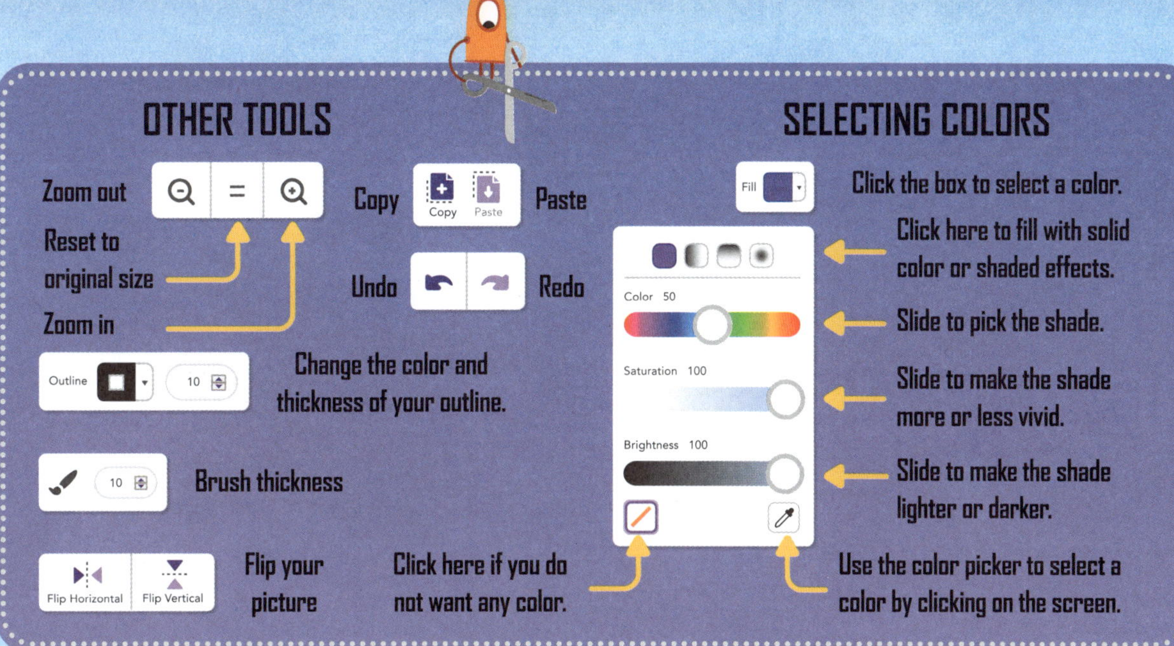

Bitmap robot

1 Click on the **brush** tool, make the line fairly thin and paint an outline. **Zoom in** for a better view of details.

2 Select the **fill** tool. Click on a color and then inside a shape to fill it in. (Make sure there are no gaps, or the color will spill out!) Click **undo** if you make a mistake.

3 To change the size, click on the **select** tool. Click and drag on screen to make a box around your picture, then drag the corners to make it bigger or smaller.

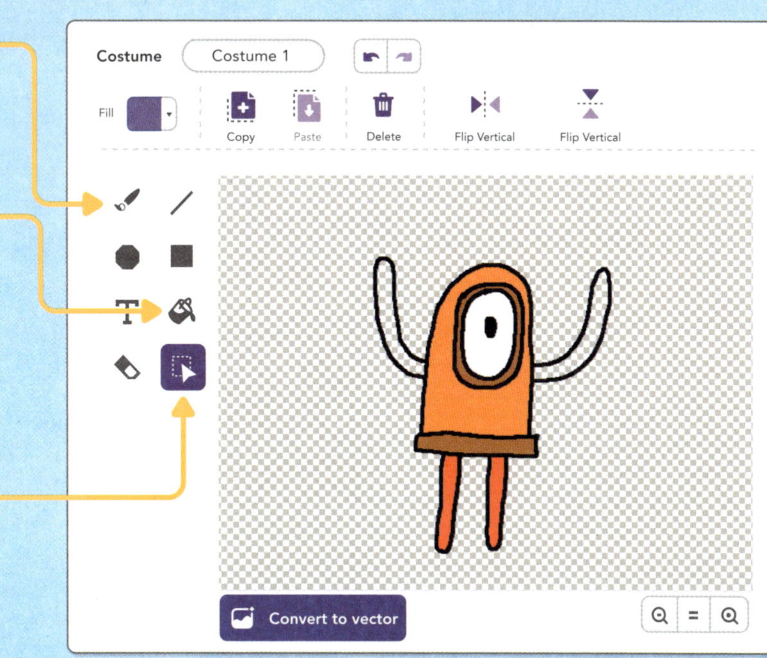

Saving your sprite

You can save the new sprite on your computer or keep it in your **Backpack** (if you have an online Scratch account), ready to use in any project. See page 80 for more about saving.

Vector race car

1 Click on the **rectangle** tool and pick a color for your car.

2 Draw a large rectangle for the car body. Add a thin rectangle over the front and a thick one at the back, like this.

3 Draw black rectangles for front and back wheels. Click on the **copy** tool and then on the wheel to make each into a pair. Use the **select** tool to position them.

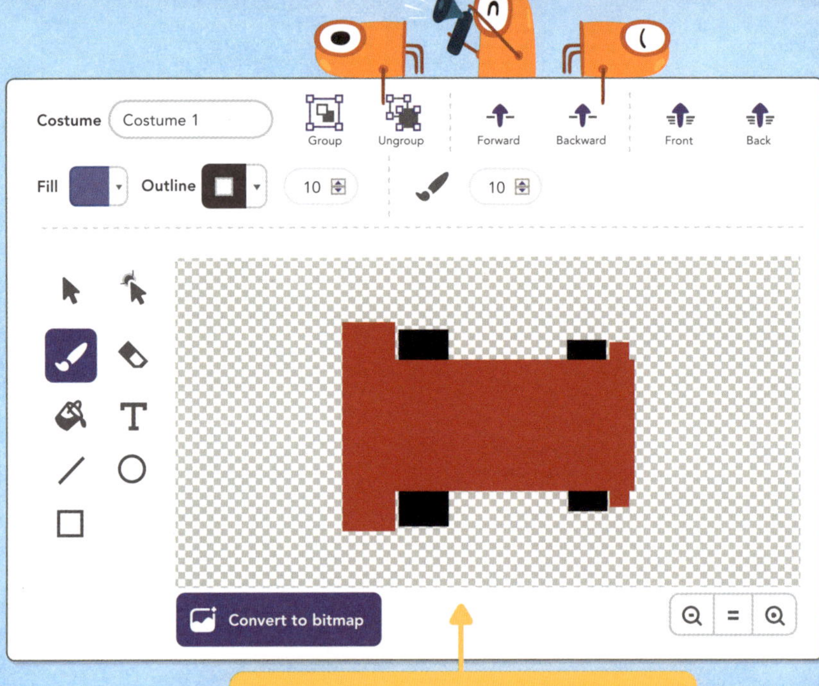

Make sure you draw your car facing right, as Scratch will assume that is the front.

Adding details

1 You could add more rectangles for a cockpit and windscreen. Use the **fill** tool to change the color of any section.

2 You could also add a driver using a round shape known as an **ellipse.** Use the **layer** buttons to place shapes in front or behind others.

3 To finish, you could add an exhaust pipe at the back.

Save the finished picture or put it in your **Backpack** so you can use it later.

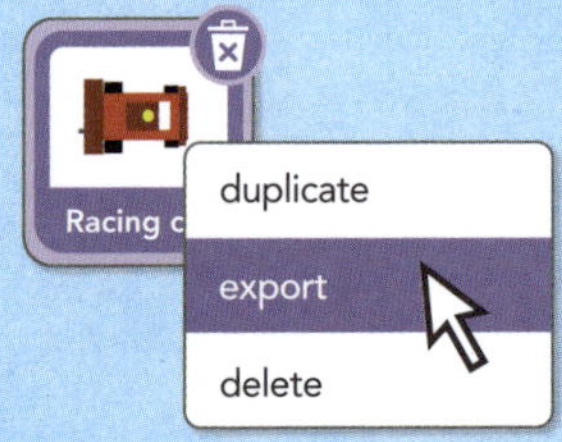

USING HOMEMADE SPRITES

The sprites on these pages will come in handy for later projects.

Alternatively, if you would like ready-made versions, you can go to **Usborne Quicklinks** to find out how to download them.

Vector monster

1 Click on the **ellipse** tool and set the fill color to 'none' (the red line). Then pick a color for the outline of your monster.

2 Start by drawing a large circle for the body and a smaller circle for the head. You can add legs using rectangles and circles.

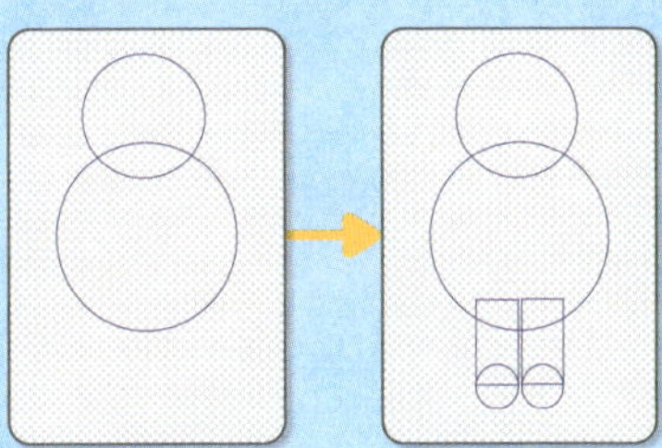

3 Select the **fill** tool and color in all the shapes. Add a white circle with a small black circle on top, to make an eye.

4 For horns, start with a green rectangle. Click on the **reshape** tool and drag the edges into a horn-shape. Use the **select** tool to select your horn, then click the **copy** tool at the top to make another horn. Click the **flip** tool at the top to flip it the other way.

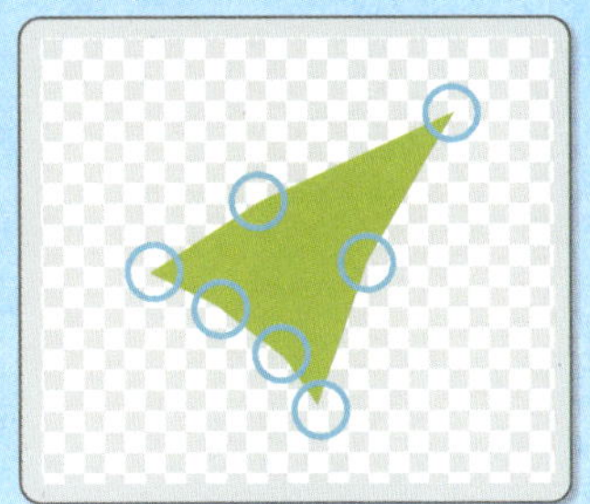

5 Click the **select** tool and drag each horn into position. To finish, you could add a mouth and arms using the **brush** tool.

Save the picture or put it in your **Backpack** so you can use it later.

CAUTION!

You can use bitmap and vector modes in the same picture – but converting a vector picture into bitmap can make the lines bumpy. Also, once converted, you won't be able to reshape things, even if you switch back to vector later.

Guess the number

Get the computer to think of a secret number, then see how quickly you can guess it.

For this game, you will need to use **Operator** blocks. Operators are used for 'operating' on or doing things with variables – especially math.

In Scratch, Operators are always snapped into other blocks, never used on their own.

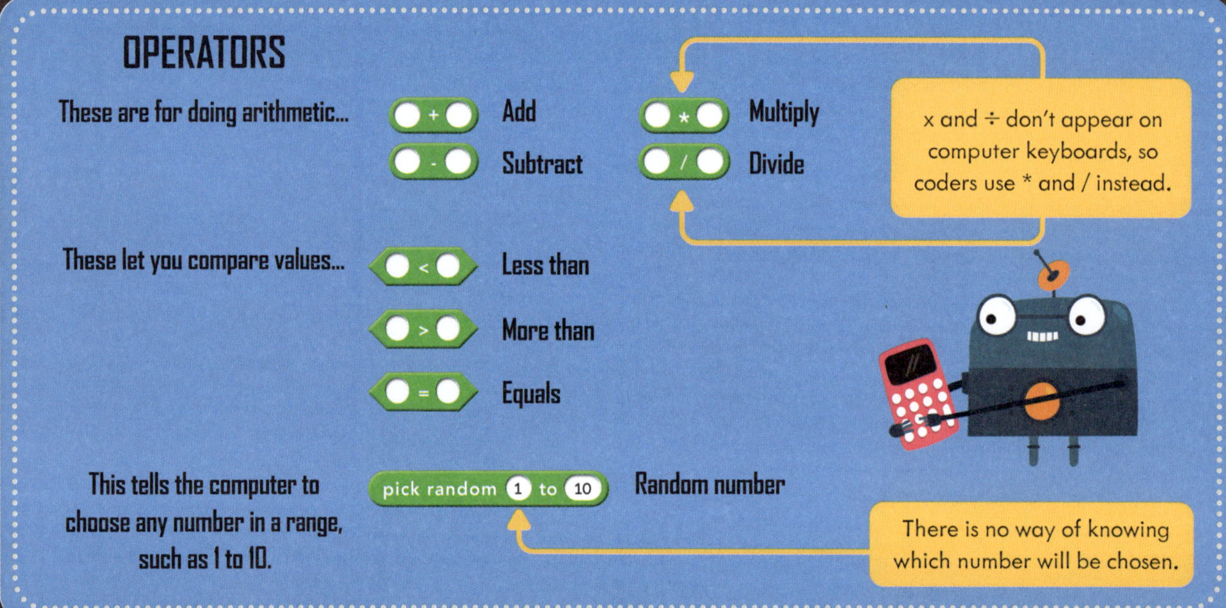

1 Start a new project, delete the cat and choose a sprite. Then go to the **Variables** menu and create a new variable called 'secret number'.

2 Tell the computer to set the secret number to a random value, each time you start the game.

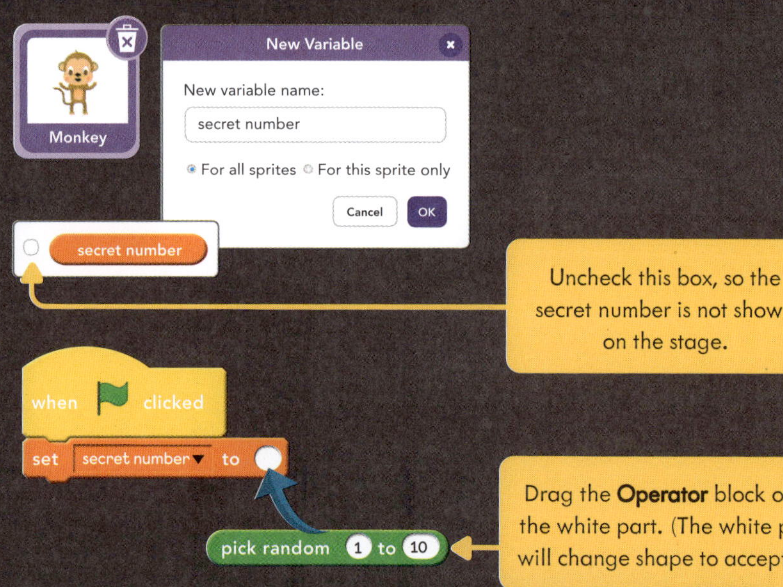

Planning your code

The next part is more complicated. So before you do any more coding, it's best to make a plan. For this, you need to work out exactly what your program needs to do, in every event.

PLANNING

Planning is something all coders do. The more organised you are before you start, the fewer bugs you will end up with.

In this case, that means...

What happens if I guess right?

What happens if my guess is too high?

What happens if my guess is too low?

You can draw out the options in a step-by-step diagram or flow chart, like this...

FLOW CHARTS

Flow charts should always be drawn in the same way, with each step in a separate box and arrows to show which way to go.

Use ovals for the START and END. Use rectangles for ordinary steps. Diamonds show there is a DECISION to make.

START

Sprite creates secret number.

Sprite asks player to guess number.

Player enters guess.

Is guess correct?

NO

Is guess too high?

YES

Sprite says "Lower!"

NO

If it's not correct and not too high, it must be too low. Sprite says "Higher!".

YES

Sprite says "Bingo!"

END

Now it's time to put your plan into action...

3 Take an **ask** block from the **Sensing** menu. Click on the white box and type your question.

Now click on the block. You should see the sprite ask your question, and an answer box appear below.

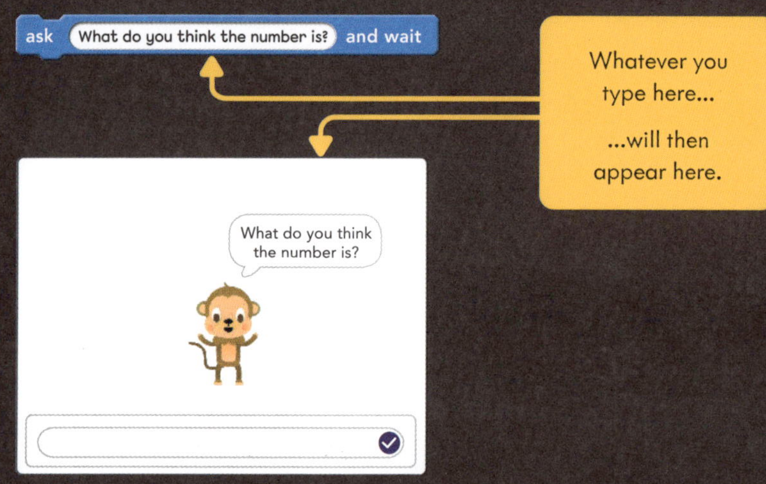

4 Take an **equals** block from the **Operators** menu. Snap in an **answer** block (from **Sensing**) on one side, and your 'secret number' variable on the other.

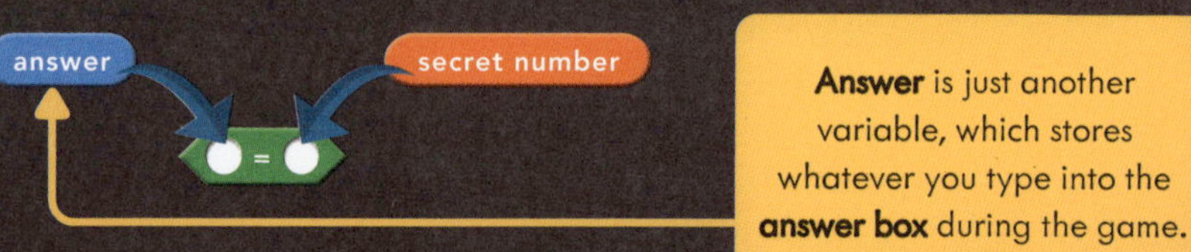

5 Snap this combined block into an **if/then** block. Now you can decide what happens *if* the answer is right.

6 Add these two blocks to say "Bingo!" and end the game if the guess matches the secret number.

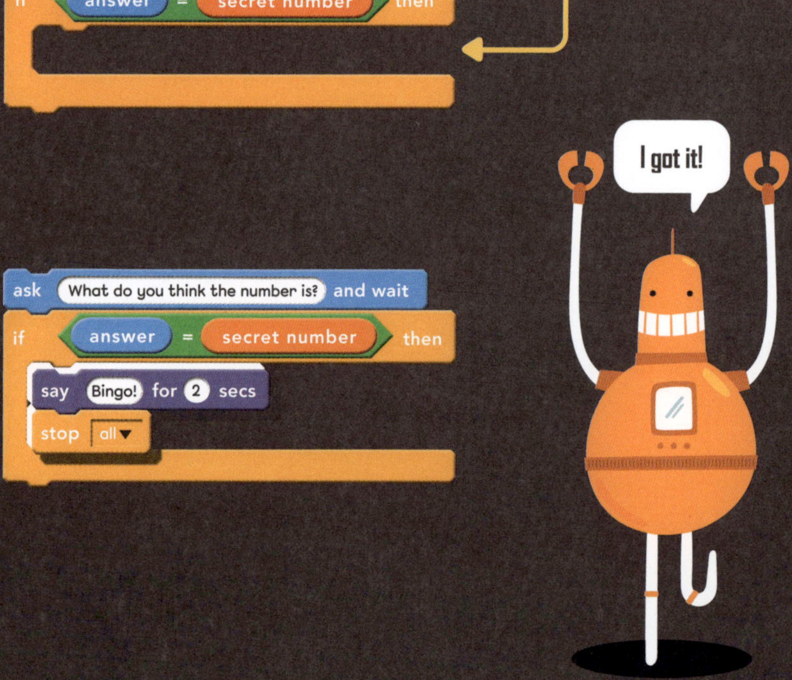

7 If the guess is wrong, use an **if/else** block to say if the secret number is higher or lower.

What happens when you guess *wrong* goes here.

Make this combined block in the same way as before, but using the **less than** block from **Operators.**

```
if answer < secret number then
    say Higher! for 2 secs
else
    say Lower! for 2 secs
```

If the answer is too low, the sprite will say *Higher!*

If the answer is not too low (and not correct) then it must be too high – so the sprite will say *Lower!*

8 Add a **repeat** loop, to decide how many attempts you get to guess the secret number.

Combine all the sections into a single script, like this, and try it out.

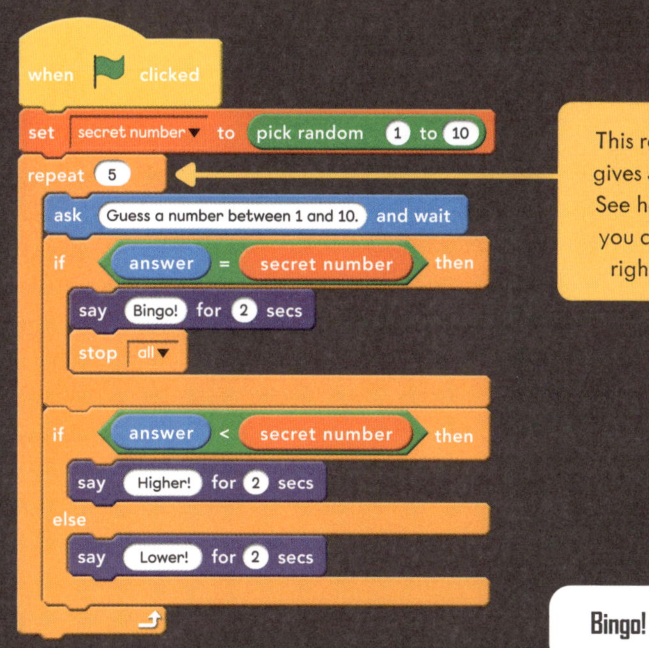

This repeat loop gives 5 attempts. See how quickly you can get the right answer.

Bat and ball

You can code two sprites to create a bat and ball game, then see how long you can keep the ball in the air.

1 Start a new project and delete the cat. Click on the **sprite** button to open the **Sprite Library** and add two new sprites.

Coding the bat

2 Select the bat in the **sprite area** and create this script to control its position. A low **y** coordinate (height) keeps the bat low on the stage. Make the **x** coordinate (left-right position) follow your mouse, using **mouse x** (from **Sensing**).

3 To make the bat look out for the ball, take an **if/then** block. Set the **if** condition with **touching** (from **Sensing**) and select 'Ball' from the drop-down menu.

4 If the bat does touch the ball, it needs to trigger a reaction. Insert a **broadcast** block (from **Events**), then add the whole stack to your **forever** loop, like this.

Coding the ball

5 Select the ball sprite. Set it to start in the middle, pointing towards the bat.

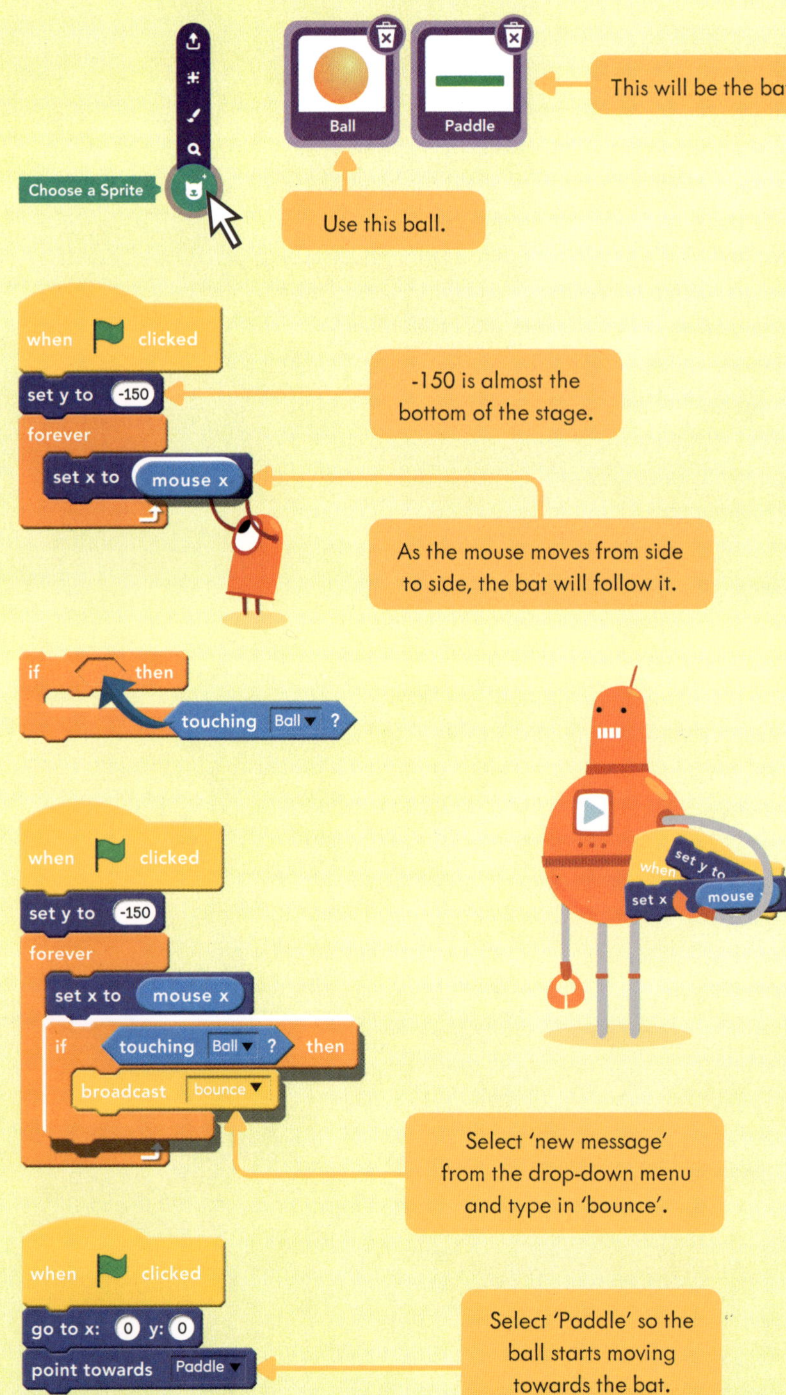

6 Add a **repeat until** loop, to keep the ball in play until you miss it. If you miss it, the **y position** will go below -150, which you can set with a **less than** block (from **Operators**).

7 Insert these two **Motion** blocks inside the loop, to keep the ball moving and make it bounce when it hits an edge.

Add a **stop all** block (from **Control**) to end the game if you miss it.

8 To make the ball react to the bat, start a new script with **when I receive.**

If the ball has hit the bat, it should bounce. Move it off the bat with a **set y** block, and send it in a new direction with **point in direction** (both from **Motion**). Use a **minus** block (from **Operators**) and a **direction** variable (**Motion**) to complete your script.

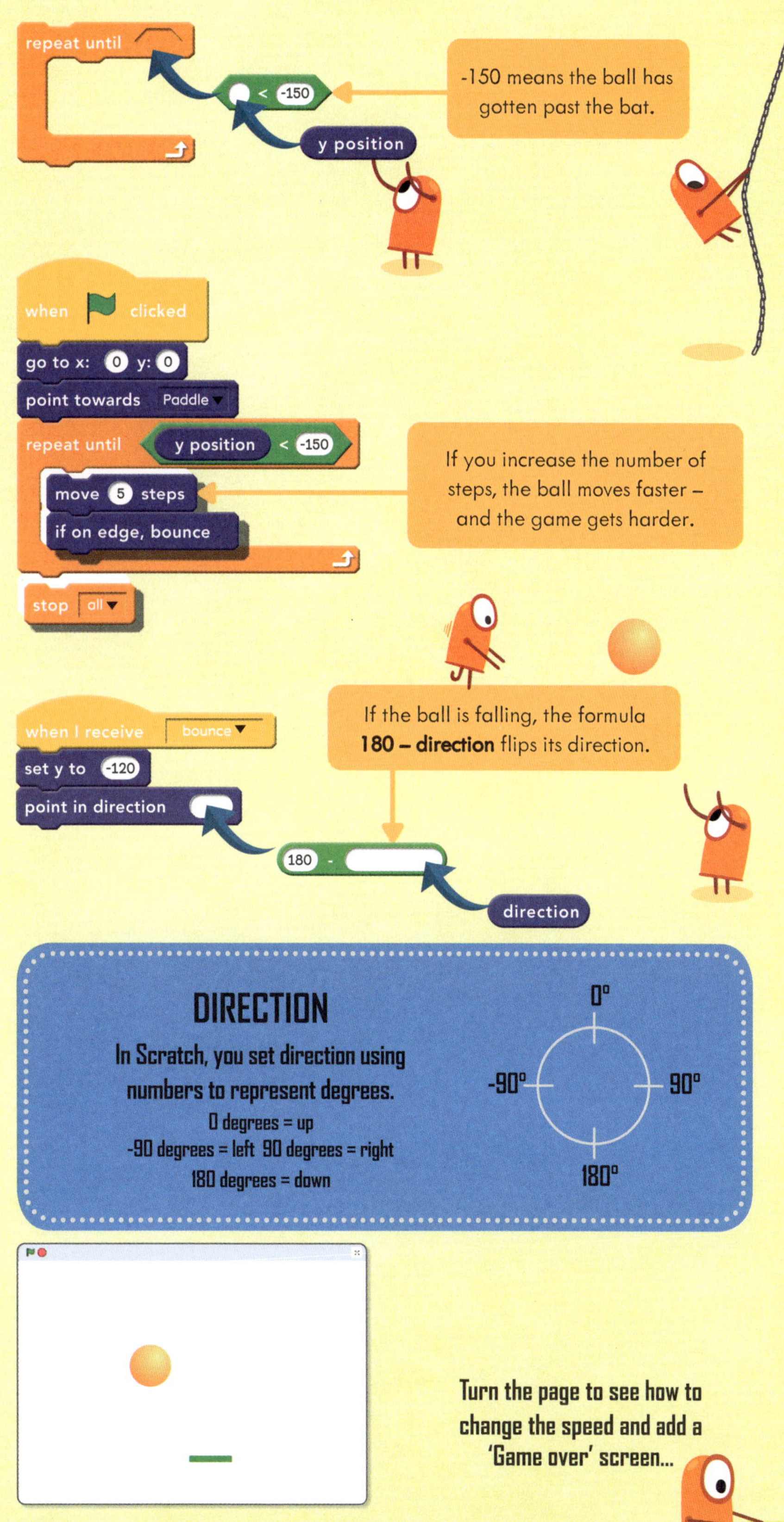

repeat until
< -150
y position
-150 means the ball has gotten past the bat.
when clicked
go to x: 0 y: 0
point towards Paddle
repeat until y position < -150
move 5 steps
if on edge, bounce
stop all
If you increase the number of steps, the ball moves faster – and the game gets harder.
when I receive bounce
set y to -120
point in direction
180 -
direction
If the ball is falling, the formula 180 – direction flips its direction.
DIRECTION
In Scratch, you set direction using numbers to represent degrees.
0 degrees = up
-90 degrees = left 90 degrees = right
180 degrees = down
0°
-90°
90°
180°

Trying it out

9 Test your code.
How long can you keep the ball bouncing around the stage?

Turn the page to see how to change the speed and add a 'Game over' screen...

Going faster

These pages show you how to make the ball speed up and add a 'Game over' screen at the end.

Making a variable

Use a **variable** to increase the speed of the ball every time it hits the bat.

1 Select the **Variables** menu and click on 'Make a Variable' (keep 'For all sprites' checked). Enter 'speed' in the pop-up window, and a set of new 'speed' variable blocks will appear.

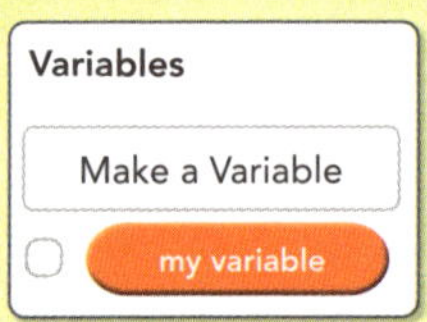

HANDLING DATA

Computers are very good at handling data (information), as long as it's labeled correctly. There are two main ways to do this: with VARIABLES, as here, and LISTS – which you will find on page 58.

Speeding up

2 Select the ball sprite. Set its starting speed by adding a **set variable** block (from **Variables**) just before the **repeat** loop in the main script.

3 To apply the speed to how the ball moves, replace the number of steps in the **move** block with a **speed** variable.

```
when [flag] clicked
go to x: (0) y: (0)
point towards [Paddle ▼]
set [speed ▼] to (5)
repeat until <(y position) < (-150)>
    move (speed) steps
    if on edge, bounce
end
stop [all ▼]
```

Select 'speed' from the drop-down menu and enter a small number to start.

Try the game now.
How long can you last before the ball gets too fast?

4 Add a **change variable** block to the **when I receive** script (and select 'speed' from the drop-down menu), so the ball gets a little faster each time it is hit.

```
when I receive [bounce ▼]
change [speed ▼] by (1)
set y to (-120)
point in direction ((180) - (direction))
```

Game over

If you like, you can add a 'Game over' screen.

1 Select the ball sprite. Replace the **stop all** with a **broadcast** block, to make the ball send a message if it hits the bottom.

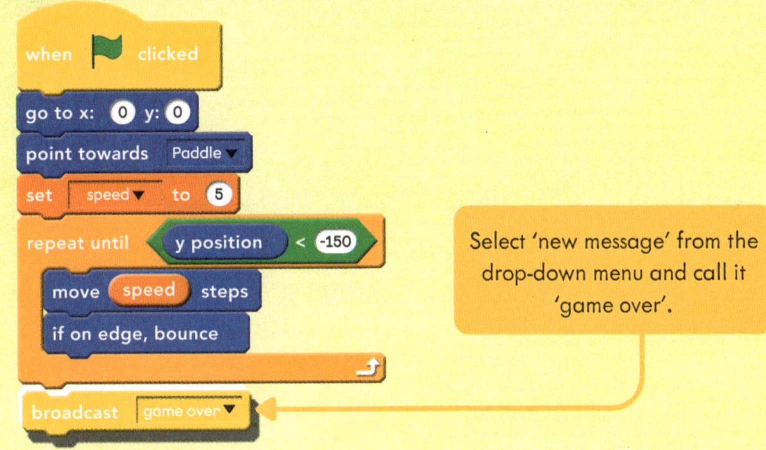

Creating a 'Game over' screen

Turn to page 32 for more about the PAINTING tools.

2 Now, create a new sprite by hovering the mouse over the **sprite** button and selecting **Paint.** This brings up the **painting tools.**

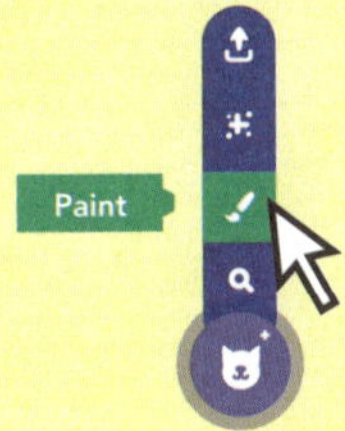

3 Click on the **T** (text tool) and then on the screen. Pick a color from the palette, and choose a type style from the drop-down menu to its left. Then type 'GAME OVER'.

GAME OVER

Click on your text and drag out the box that appears, to change the text size.

Adding the script

4 Make sure the new sprite is selected in the **sprite area**, then click on the **Code** tab. Use a **hide** block to hide the sprite when the game starts.

5 Create another script, telling the sprite to show itself when it receives the 'game over' message.

6 Add a **repeat** loop, with **change effect** and **wait** blocks, to make the sprite flash. Finish with a **stop all.**

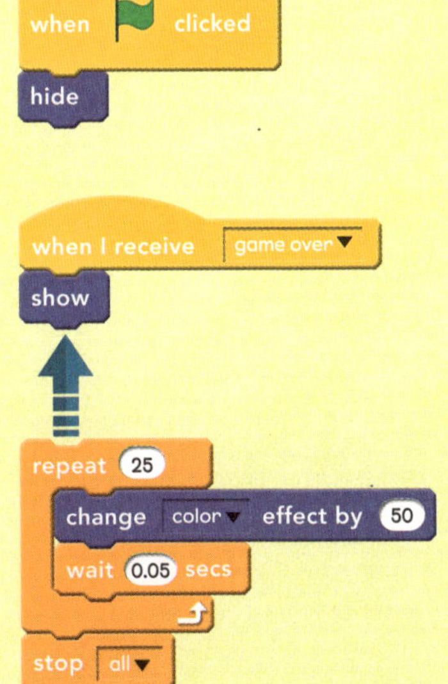

CHANGING COLORS

In Scratch, each color has a particular number – so changing the number changes the color.

Pattern maker

You can make identical copies of sprites, called **clones,** and use them to create neat, repeating patterns.

1 Start a new project, delete the cat and select a simple sprite. Find **'size'** on the **sprite menu** and make the number smaller to shrink the sprite.

2 Begin with these blocks, to send the sprite to the middle, facing right, and clear the stage each time you click on the green flag. The **erase all** block can be found in the **Pen Extension** (see page 22).

Creating clones

3 Go to **Control** and take a **create clone** block. Select 'myself' from the drop-down menu. Insert this in a **repeat** loop, to make 8 identical clones, and add it to the end of your script.

4 Then add a **hide** block (from **Looks**) to make the original sprite disappear, so you only see the clones.

5 To control the clones, you will need to number them – and make sure the numbers always start from 0.

Go to **Variables** and make a new variable called 'clone number' (select 'For all sprites' and uncheck the box so it won't show on stage). Then insert a **set variable** just after the start, like this.

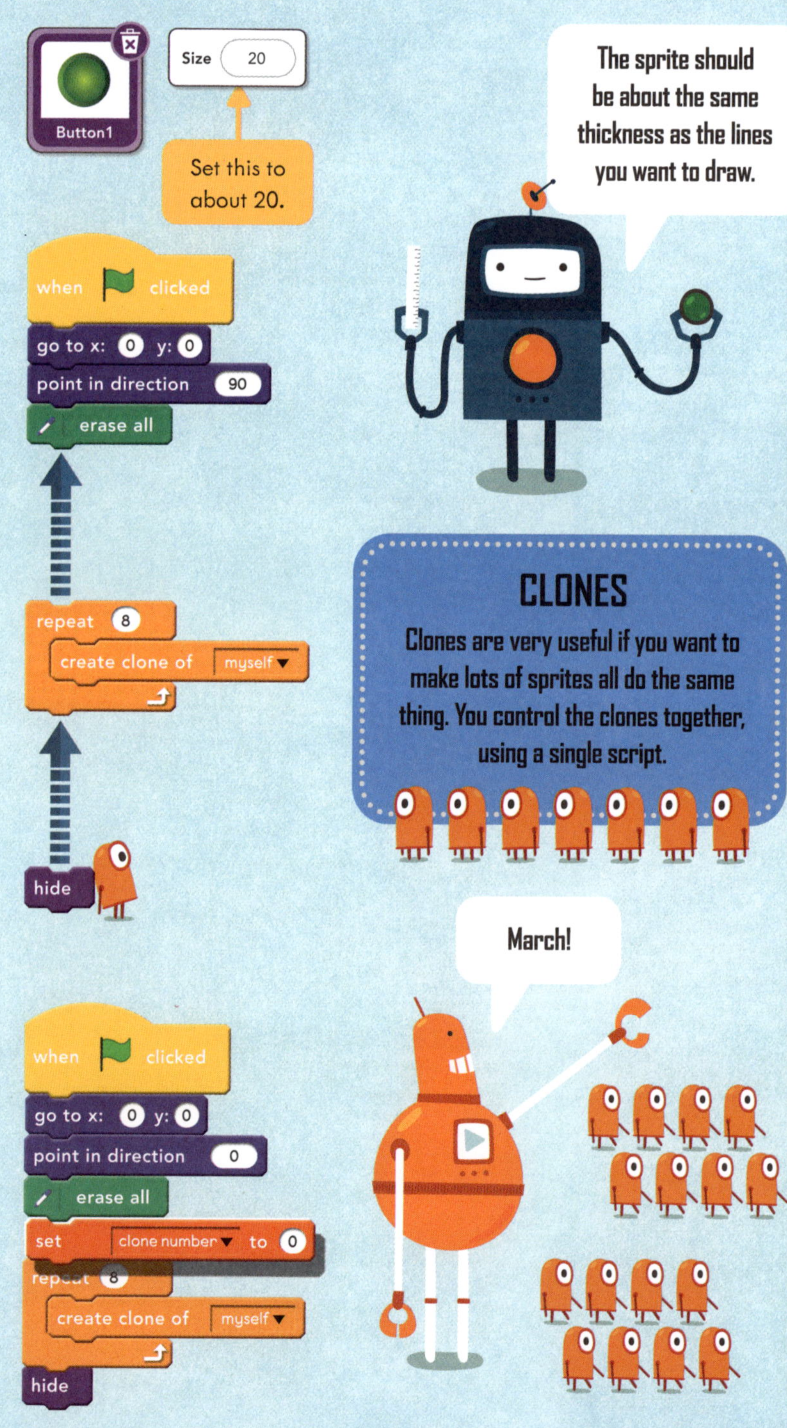

Controlling your clones

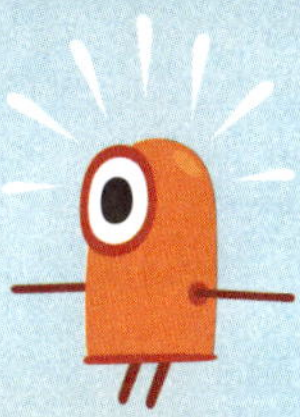

1 Start a new script with **when I start as a clone** (from **Control**). All the clones will follow these instructions when they appear – starting with a **show** block (from **Looks**).

2 Begin by arranging your clones. Take a **multiply** block (from **Operators**) and snap in **clone number.** Snap this into a **turn** block (from **Motion**) and add a **move.**

3 Add a **change variable** block, so each additional clone gets a new number.

Now to make them draw...

4 Below, add a **forever** loop with an **if/then** block inside it (both from **Control**). Set the **if** condition with **key pressed** (from **Sensing**) and select 'up arrow'. Then insert **move, stamp** (from the **Pen Extension**) and **change effect** (**Looks**).

5 For sideways controls, insert two more **if/then** blocks inside the **forever** loop. Snap in **key pressed** blocks for left and right arrows, and add **turn** blocks (from **Motion**), like this.

Click on the green flag to try out the finished script...

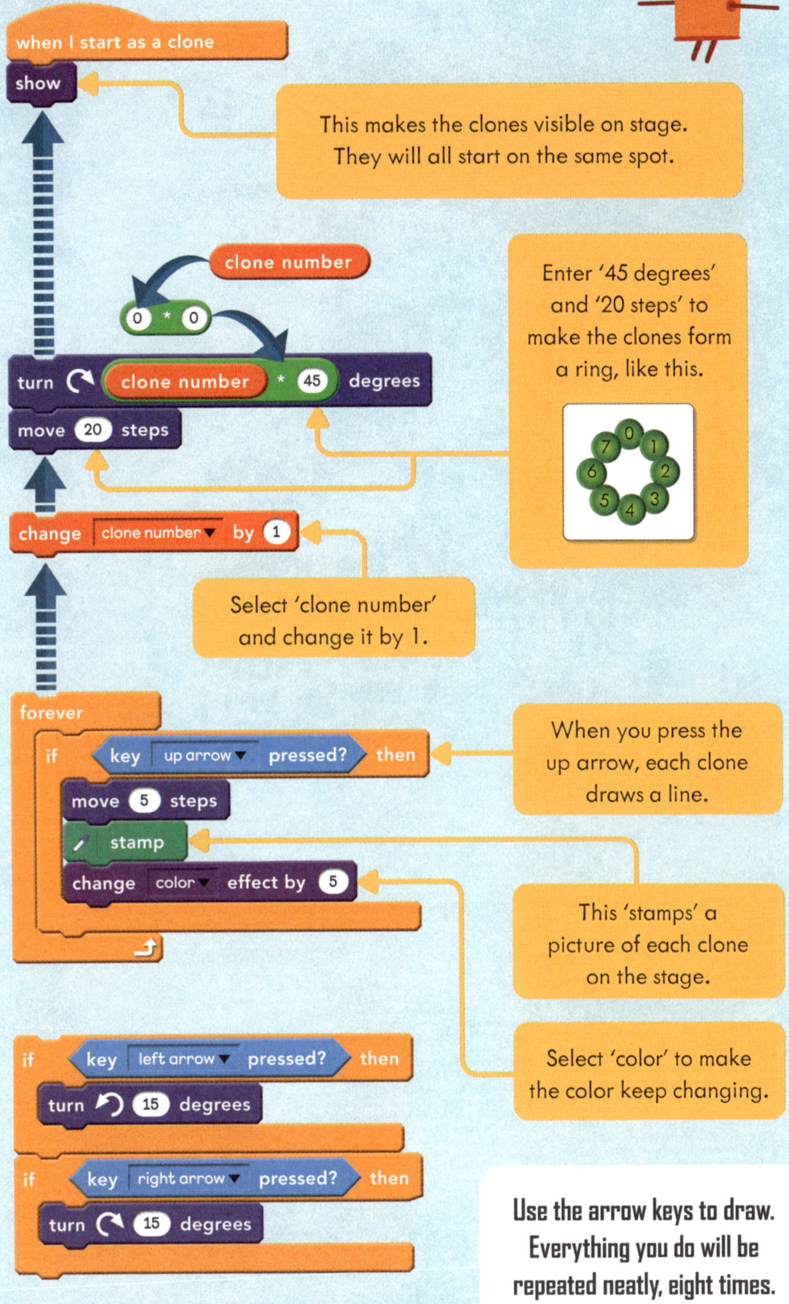

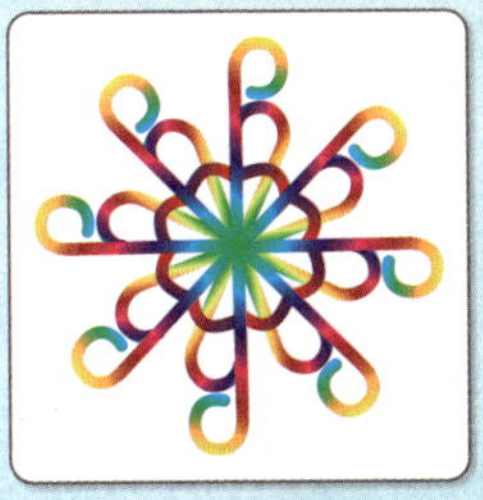

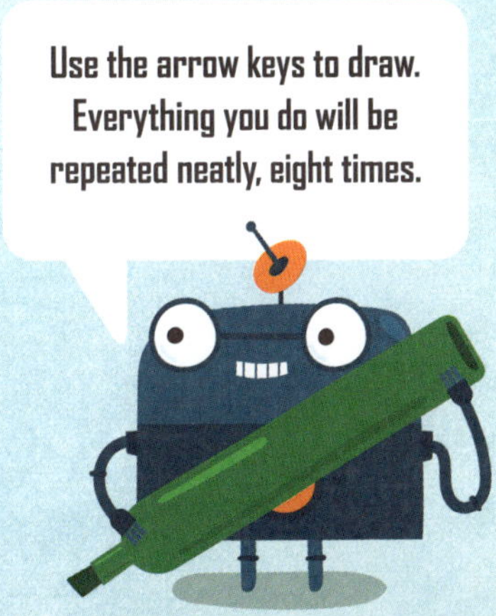

```
when I start as a clone
show
turn ↻ (clone number * 45) degrees
move 20 steps
change [clone number ▾] by 1
forever
  if <key [up arrow ▾] pressed?> then
    move 5 steps
    stamp
    change [color ▾] effect by 5
  if <key [left arrow ▾] pressed?> then
    turn ↺ 15 degrees
  if <key [right arrow ▾] pressed?> then
    turn ↻ 15 degrees
```

clone number

(0) * (0)

This makes the clones visible on stage. They will all start on the same spot.

Enter '45 degrees' and '20 steps' to make the clones form a ring, like this.

Select 'clone number' and change it by 1.

When you press the up arrow, each clone draws a line.

This 'stamps' a picture of each clone on the stage.

Select 'color' to make the color keep changing.

Use the arrow keys to draw. Everything you do will be repeated neatly, eight times.

Virtual pet

Scratch makes it possible to create your very own virtual pet, and keep it entertained.

Create a pet

1 Start a new project, delete the cat and choose a sprite to be your pet. You could draw your own or use a ready-made one. (If you want to use ours, go to **Usborne Quicklinks** for instructions.) Don't forget to include the sprite's costumes (see the list on the right) too.

2 Add a backdrop to give your pet a home – you could upload one of your own, or use a ready-made one.

3 To make sure your pet starts in the right costume, in the right place, use a **green flag** followed by **switch costume to** (from **Looks**), and **go to** (from **Motion**).

Feeding time

1 Add another sprite to be your pet's food. Drag it to one corner of the stage. Make a note of its coordinates (shown below the stage) for step 3 on the next page.

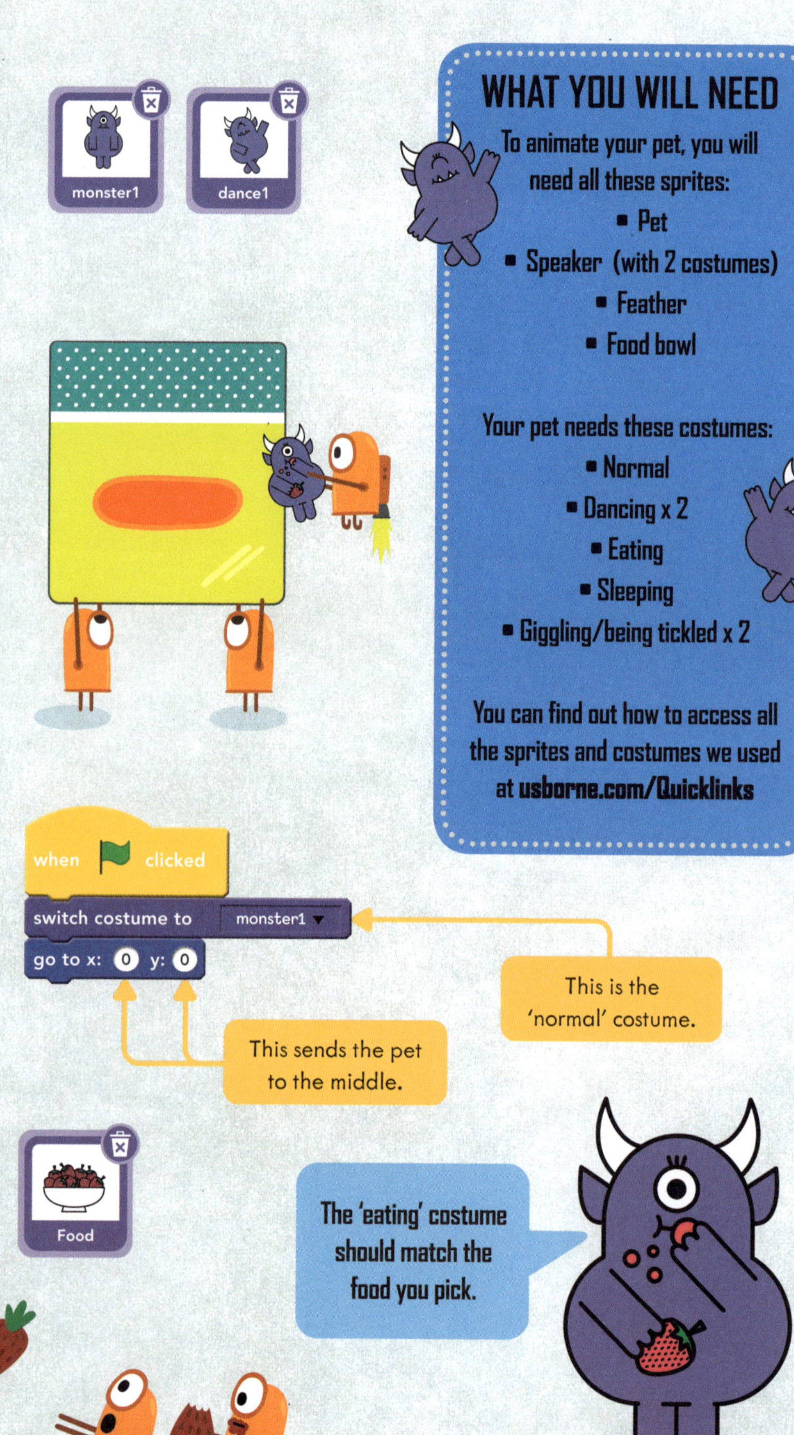

2 Select the food in the **sprite area**, go to **Events** and create this script. In the **broadcast** block, select 'new message' and call it 'come eat'.

3 Select your pet in the **sprite area** and start a new script with **when I receive.** Add a **glide** block (from **Motion**) to make it go to the food.

4 When the pet reaches its food, use a **switch costume** block to show it eating. You could add a **say** block and a sound, too. (Remember to select the sound in the **Sounds Library** as well as adding **start sound.**)

5 Then, switch back to the pet's original costume and send it back to its starting position.

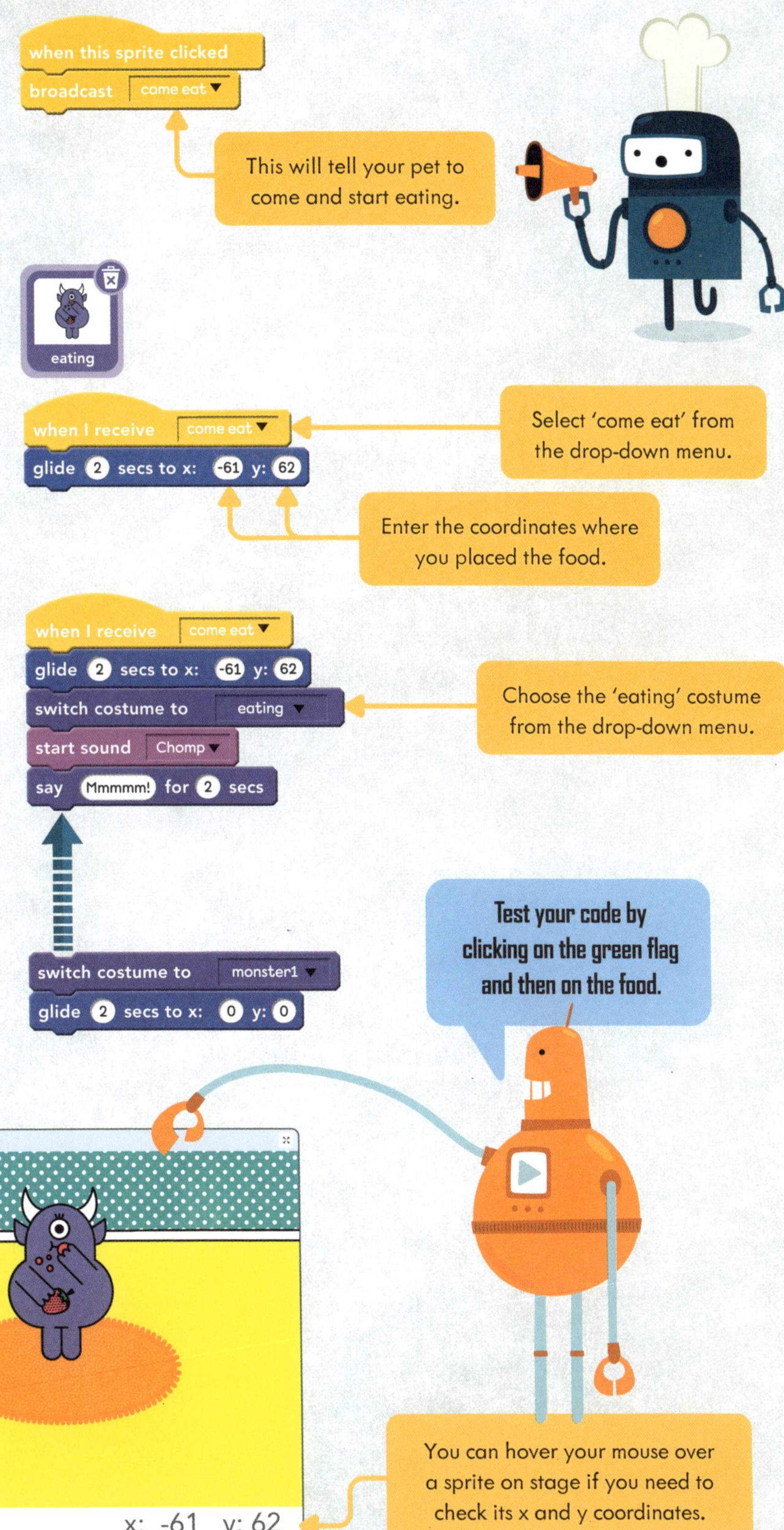

Tickling

1 To tickle your pet, add another sprite – we used a feather. Drag it into another corner of the stage.

Feather
You could draw your own feather, or get one from the Usborne library.
when this sprite clicked
broadcast tickle

2 Select the feather in the **sprite area**, go to **Events** and create this script. In the **broadcast** block, select 'new message' and call it 'tickle'.

3 Go back to your pet and start a new script with **when I receive** followed by **glide**, to make the pet move over to the feather. Then add a **switch costume** block.

4 Add a laugh with **start sound**, then **wait** and **switch costume** again. Add another laugh, **wait** and **switch costume** to the original. Then, send your pet back to the start.

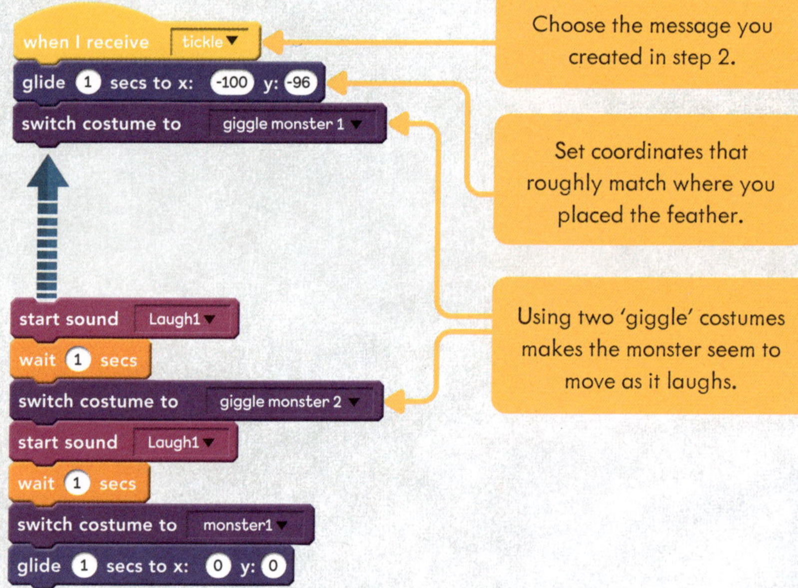

Let's dance

1 For dancing, add a musical sprite – we drew a speaker and gave it an extra costume with 'noise' lines. Drag this to another corner of the stage.

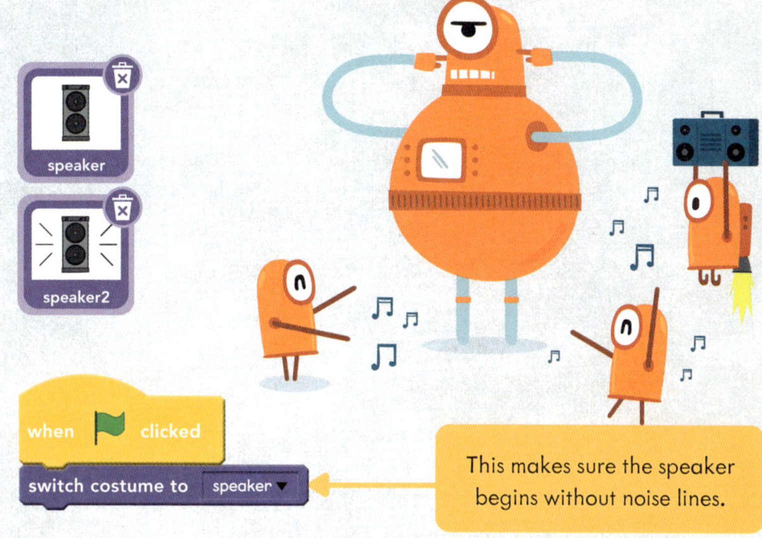

2 Select the speaker in the **sprite area** and start a new script like this.

3 With the speaker still selected, start another script to broadcast a new message called 'come dance'.

4 For the music, add a **play sound** block and choose some music from the **Sounds Library.** Finish by broadcasting 'stop dancing'.

5 To make the speaker show it's playing, start another script with **when I receive,** followed by a **forever** loop of alternate **wait** and **switch costume** blocks.

6 Add a short script like this, to make the music and dancing stop at the same time.

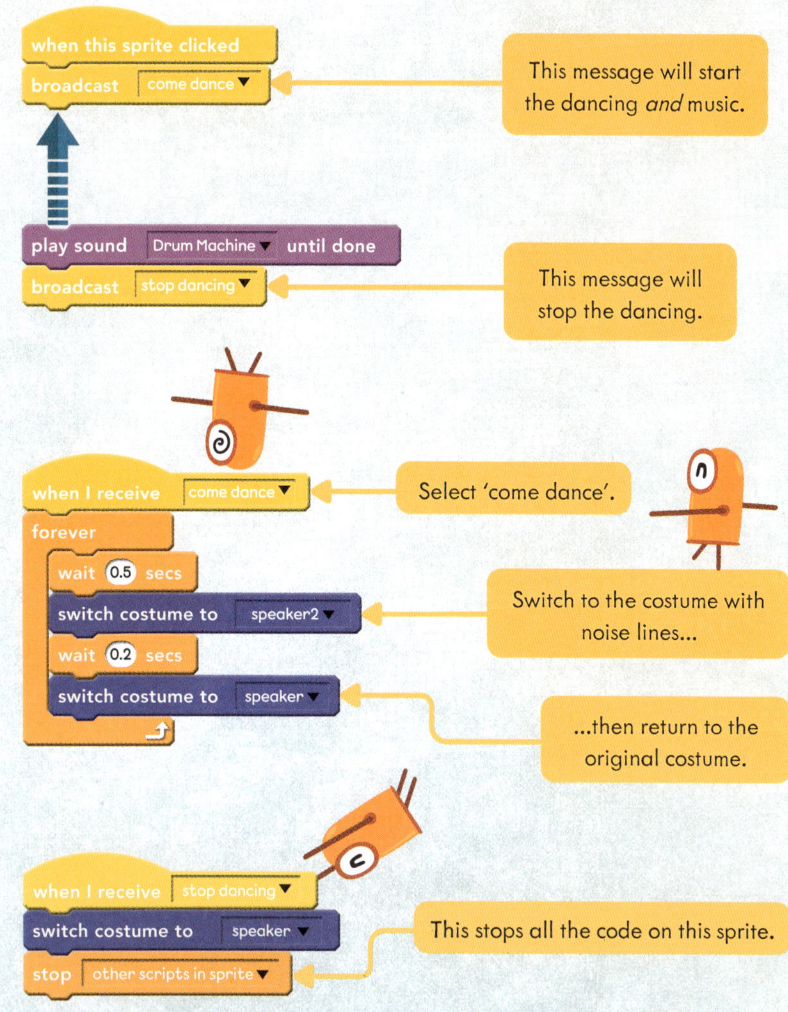

7 To make your pet dance, select the pet in the **sprite area** and create a new script, like this. Wrap a **forever** loop around the costume switches, to keep the dance going.

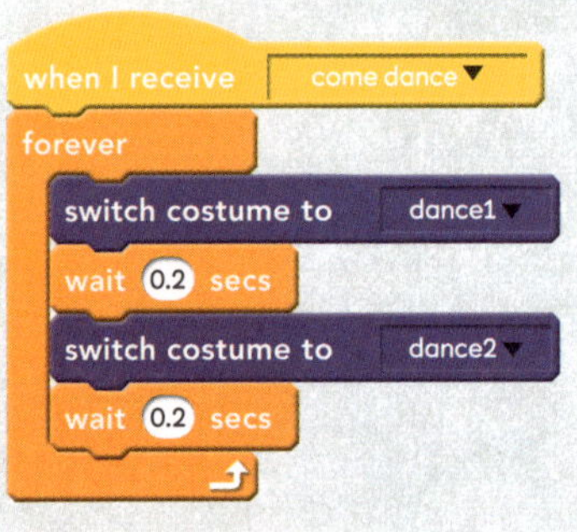

8 Lastly, create a short script like this, to make the dance stop at the same time as the music. Test your code by clicking on the speaker.

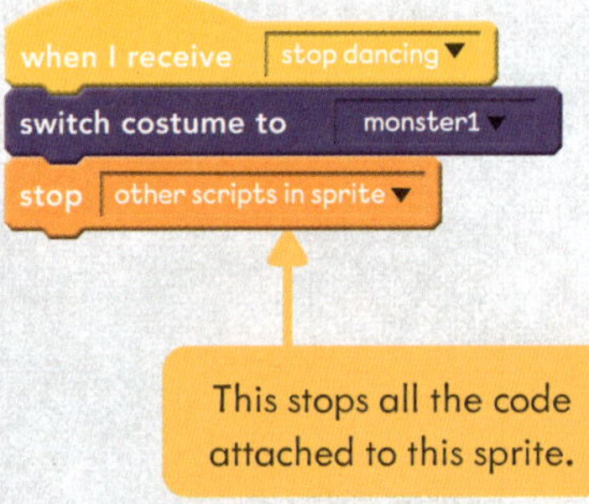

WARNING: if you ask your pet to do two things at once, it may get confused. If this happens, just press the green flag to restart.

Bedtime

1 To make your pet fall asleep on the spot, select the pet in the **sprite area** and start a new script with **when key pressed**. Then add **switch costume to** and select 'sleeping'.

when space key pressed
switch costume to sleeping

We chose the space bar, but you could use any key from the drop-down menu.

2 To make your pet snore, add a **repeat** loop with **start sound** and **say** blocks, like this.

Finish with **switch costume**, to wake it up again.

This sounds like snoring – or you could record your own sound effect.

Test your code by pressing the space bar.

Give your pet a voice

1 To make your pet make a noise when you click on it, select your pet sprite and start a new script with **when this sprite clicked**.

2 Go to **Variables** and make a new **variable** called 'noise' (make it 'For all sprites' and uncheck the box so it won't show on stage). Then take a **set variable** block and snap in **pick random** (from **Operators**).

You can scroll around the SCRIPT AREA if there is too much code to see all at once.

3 For each noise, take an **if/then** block. Set the condition with an **equals** block (from **Operators**), so the noise plays when you get a particular random number.

4 If you like, you can 'translate' the noise by adding a **think** block, too.

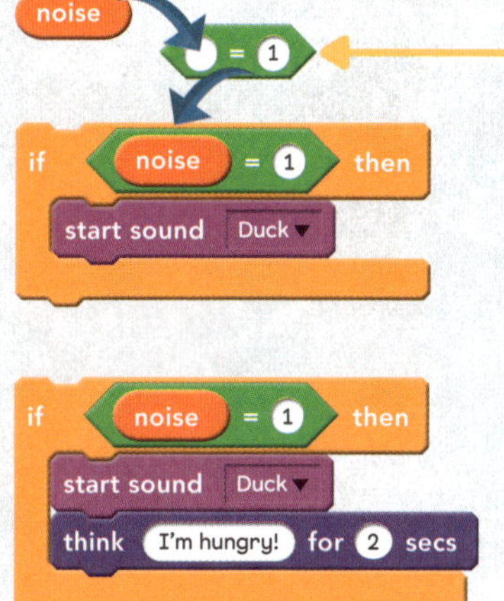

The numbers will represent the different noises your pet can make.

ADDING SOUNDS

You could record a sound, or use one from the Scratch library. Remember, each new sound must be added in the SOUNDS LIBRARY before it will play.

5 Add a few different sounds, like this. Test your code by clicking on your pet a few times.

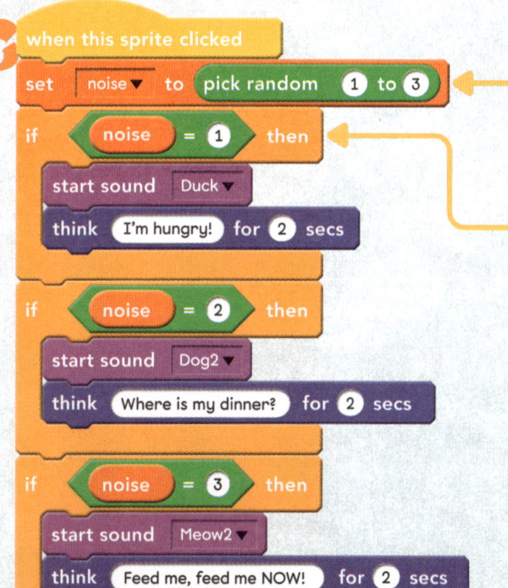

This range should match the number of noises you've added.

Give each noise a number.

QUICKLINKS

You can meet our pet by going to **Usborne Quicklinks**.

Games

Once you have mastered the basics of Scratch, you can practice your coding skills with these advanced games. The games build on what you did earlier, so make sure you have worked through the main section of the book *before* you start.

Each game comes with an online 'starter pack' of ready-made sprites and backdrops for you to use. You will find links to all the packs, along with our versions of the game scripts, at **usborne.com/Quicklinks**

Race car

Create a race car and track,
with a board to display your lap times.

Design phase

1 Start a new project and delete the cat. Then, design your track. Hover the mouse over the **backdrop** button (below the stage) and select **Paint** to bring up the **painting tools.**

Use the **paint can** to make the **stage** green. Select a thick gray **brush** to draw the track. Use a thin brush in a *new* color for the finish line.

2 Find the car sprite you made on page 34 and add it. (If you have a Scratch account, drag it out of your **Backpack.** If you don't, hover over the **sprite** button and select **Upload** to upload it from your computer). The car will now appear on the stage *and* in the **sprite area.**

On the grid

3 Drag the car to the start (it must be in front of the line but not touching it). Click on the car in the **sprite area.** Use the spinner to make it point the right way and change its size to '55'. Make a note of the numbers for **x, y** and **direction.**

Start a script with the **green flag** block. Add **point in direction** and **go to** (both from **Motion**) and enter the numbers you noted.

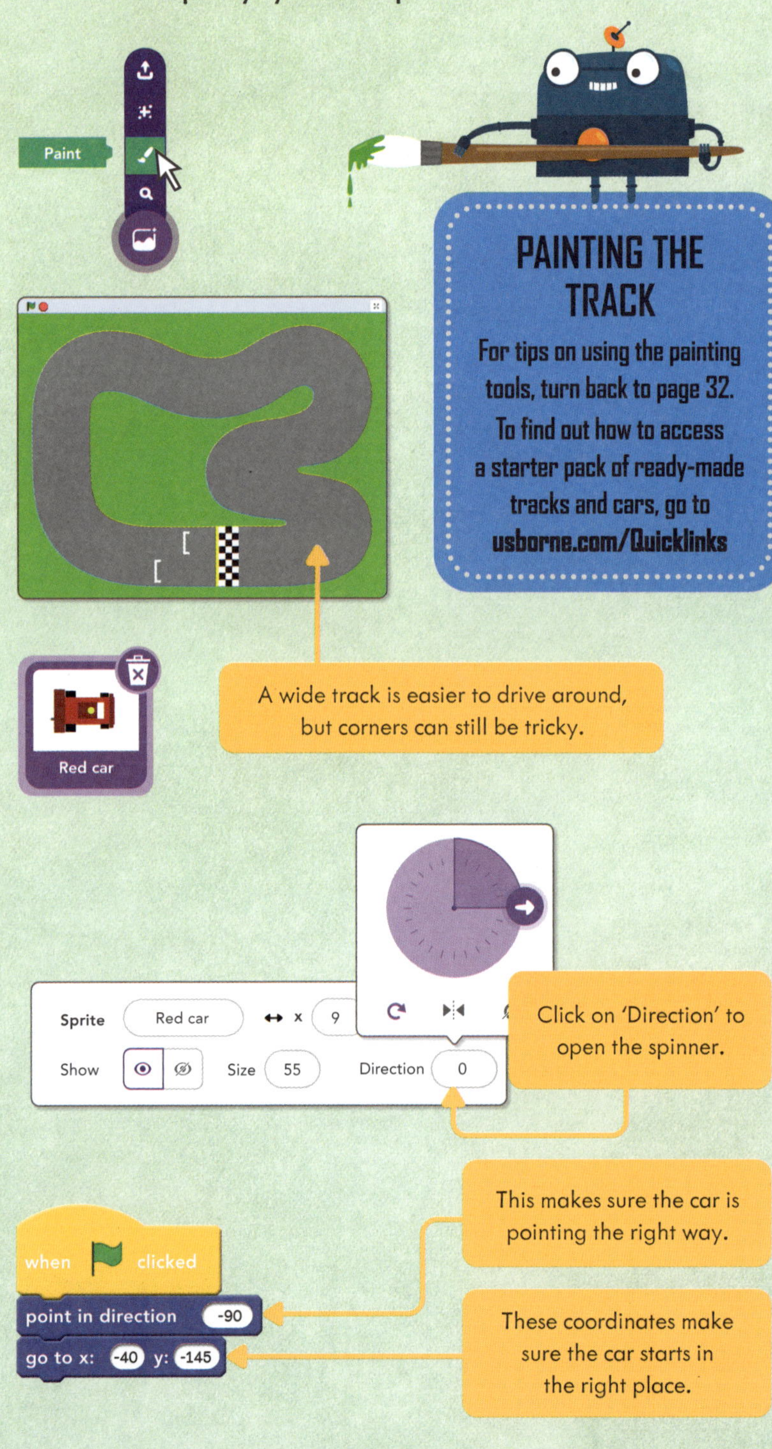

Paint
PAINTING THE TRACK
For tips on using the painting tools, turn back to page 32.
To find out how to access a starter pack of ready-made tracks and cars, go to usborne.com/Quicklinks
Red car
A wide track is easier to drive around, but corners can still be tricky.
Sprite
Red car
x
9
Show
Size
55
Direction
0
Click on 'Direction' to open the spinner.
when clicked
point in direction -90
go to x: -40 y: -145
This makes sure the car is pointing the right way.
These coordinates make sure the car starts in the right place.

Starting the clock

4 To time your lap, go to the **Variables** menu and select 'Make a Variable'. Call the new variable 'lap time'.

5 Drag a **set variable** block into the **script area** and select 'lap time' from the drop-down menu. Slot a **timer** (from **Sensing**) into the white bit.

6 Wrap a **repeat until** loop around it. Set the condition with **touching color**, so the timer counts until you cross the finish.

7 Add the **repeat until** loop below the script from step 3. Then insert a **reset timer** block (from **Sensing**) just below the start. This ensures the timer will always start from zero.

Steering

8 You can steer the car with the arrow keys. Go to the **Sensing** menu and select a **key pressed** block.

Snap it into an **if/then** block and select 'right arrow' from the drop-down menu. Then insert a **turn right** block (from **Motion**).

Repeat with a second **if/then** block, selecting 'left arrow' and a **turn left** block.

Insert both **if/then** blocks into the **repeat until** loop (below **set lap time**) from step 7.

You can see the finished script on page 57.

Picking up speed

9 To control the car's speed, you need another **variable.** Call it 'speed' and uncheck the box so it won't be shown. Add a **set variable** block at the start, to ensure it starts from 0.

10 Take an **if/then** and another **key pressed**, but this time select 'up arrow'. Use **change variable** to increase the speed if this key is pressed.

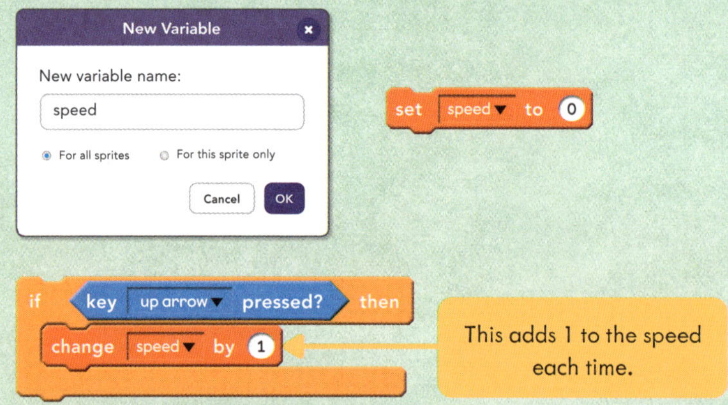

Slowing down

Race cars don't just speed up – they also have an effect known as 'drag' which slows them down. You get some drag all the time, even driving on a race track, but a lot more if you drive over grass...

SMOOTH SLOWDOWNS

A handy trick for slowing down, often used in games, is to MULTIPLY the speed by LESS THAN 1. This reduces the speed gradually, creating a smooth, realistic slowdown. It's a good way to mimic the effects of drag (see also page 69).

11 Take an **if/else** block and set the 'if' condition with **touching color**, to detect if the car goes off track.

If it does, **set speed** to **speed** multiplied by 0.5 (with a **multiply** block from **Operators**) to apply drag.

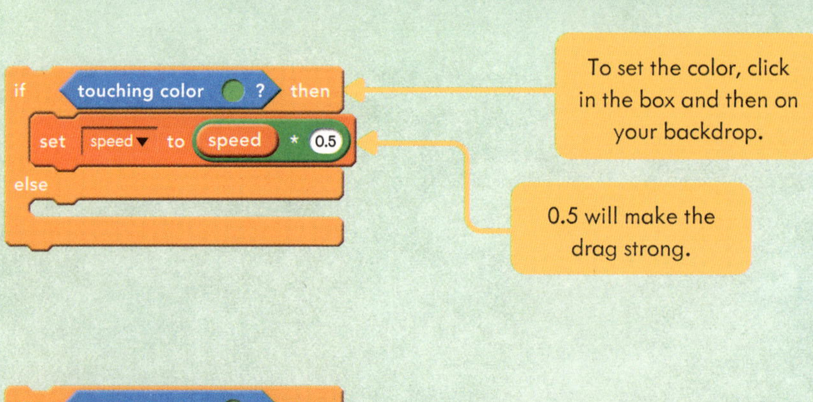

12 When the car is on the track, there should be less drag. Under 'else', **set speed** to **speed** multiplied by 0.8. Then add a **move** block, and set it to **speed** steps.

Add the whole stack inside the **repeat** loop from step 7.

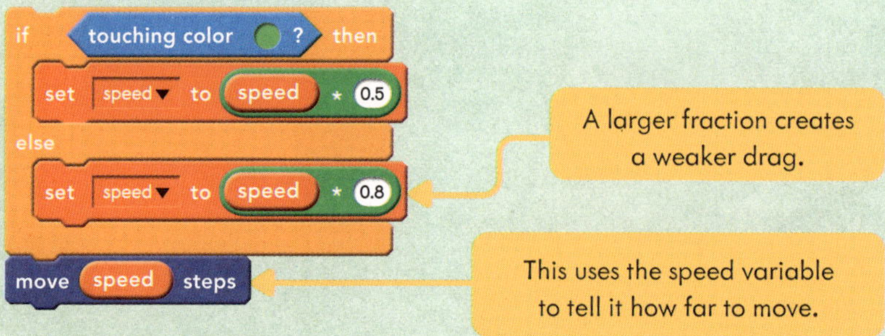

13 You could also add a sound at the end, below the loop, to celebrate finishing.

start sound Gong

Ready, set, go!

14 Click the green flag to start the game and see how fast you can drive around the track.

If it doesn't work, there must be a bug in the code. Double-check it against the script below.

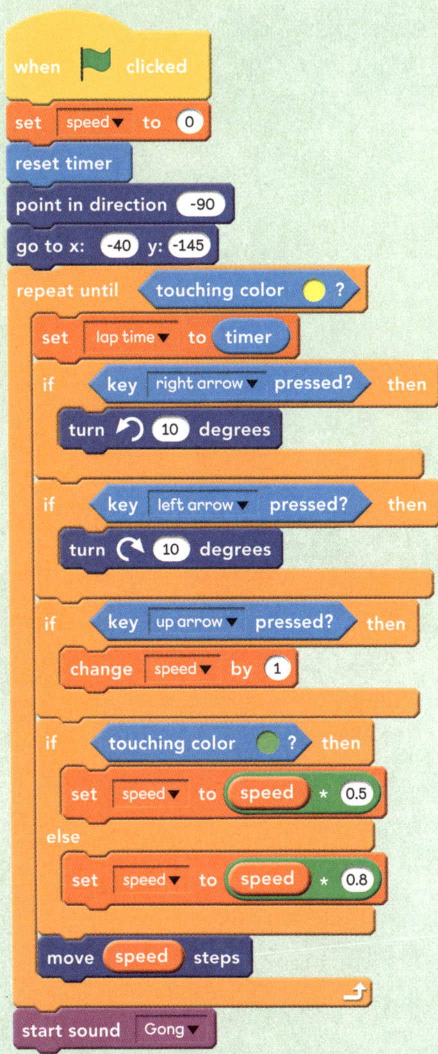

LOTS OF BLOCKS

As your scripts get longer and more complicated, it gets harder to follow what's happening. Remember always to read the blocks in order, from top to bottom, and from left to right – just like your computer.

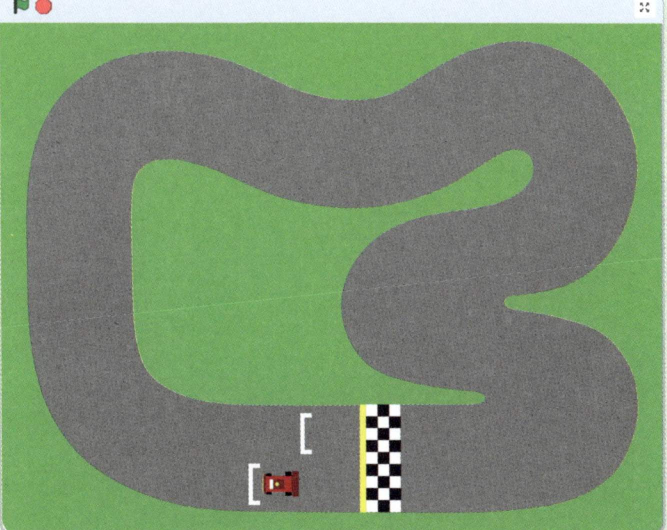

Lap time list

1 You can also record your lap times. First, insert a **broadcast** block below the **start sound** block from step 13. This sends a message when you finish a lap.

2 Then start a new script with **when I receive.** (This will activate when you cross the finish.)

3 To store the times, you need to make a **list**. Go to **Variables** and select 'Make a List'. Call it 'lap times' and uncheck the box, so it doesn't show on stage during the game.

4 To add lap times to the list, take an **add... to** block (from **Variables**). Snap a **lap time** variable into the white box, and select 'lap times' from the drop-down menu.

5 Then add a **show list** block to your new script, and select 'lap times' from the menu again. This will reveal the list when the game finishes.

6 To hide the list when you start a new lap, take another **green flag** block and add **hide list** (from **Variables**), like this.

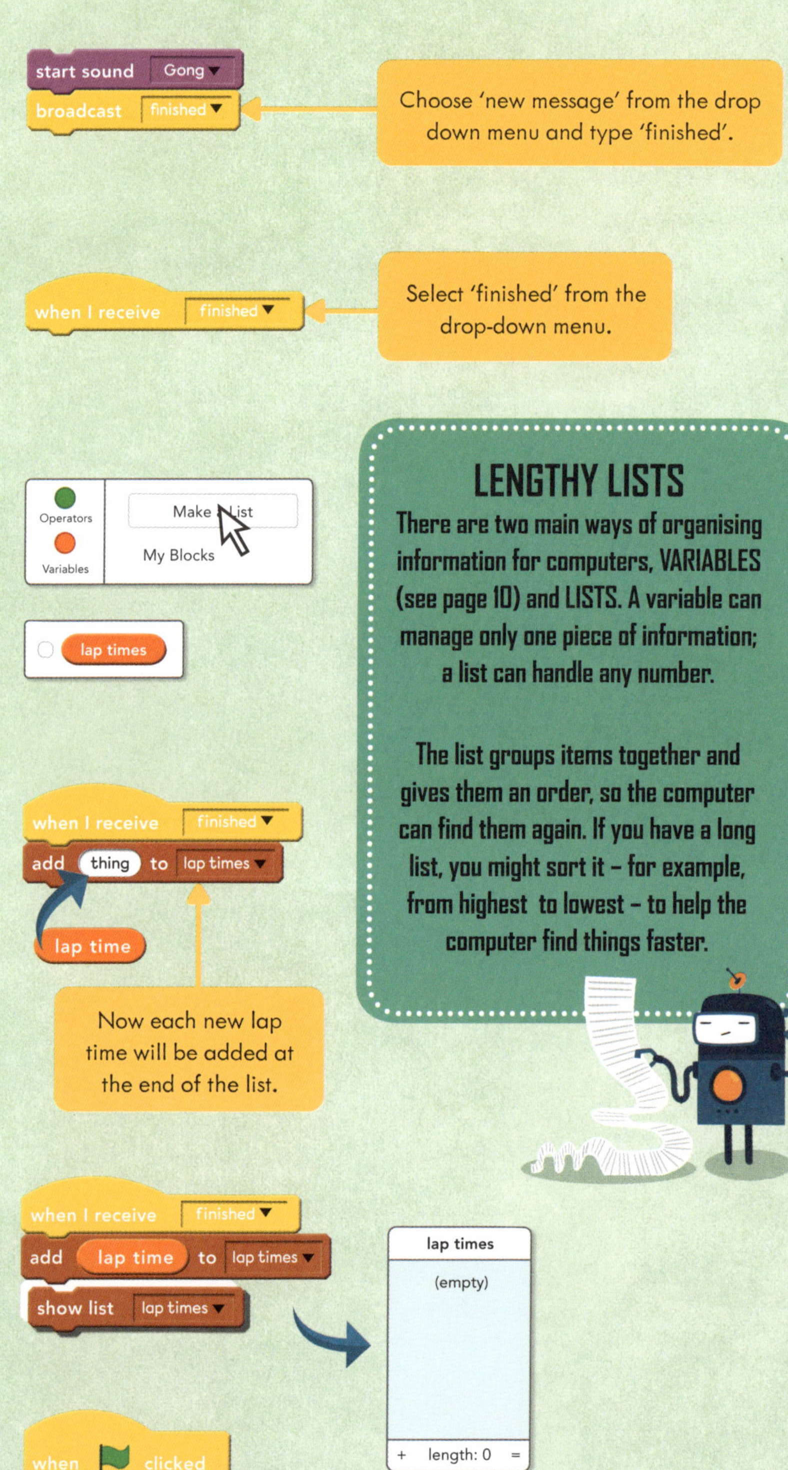

LENGTHY LISTS

There are two main ways of organising information for computers, VARIABLES (see page 10) and LISTS. A variable can manage only one piece of information; a list can handle any number.

The list groups items together and gives them an order, so the computer can find them again. If you have a long list, you might sort it – for example, from highest to lowest – to help the computer find things faster.

Who's the fastest?

If you like, you can record player names alongside lap times, so you can challenge your friends and see who's the fastest.

1 Make a new list, called 'names'.

2 Take an **ask** block (from **Sensing**) and insert it below **when I receive** (from step 2 on the previous page). This will ask the player's name at the end of a lap.

3 Take an **answer** variable (from **Sensing**) and slot it into an **add... to** block (from **Variables**). Select 'names' from the drop-down menu, and insert it below the **ask** block.

4 Insert another **show list** block, to make the names appear alongside the lap times. Your finished script should look like this.

5 Lastly, add another **hide list** to the script from step 7 on the previous page. This makes sure *both* lists are hidden when you start a new lap.

Space adventure

In this game, you steer a spaceship through space — but watch out for asteroids and other obstacles!

1 Start a new project, delete the cat and add two new sprites: a spaceship and an asteroid. (We used sprites from the Usborne starter pack.)

Spaceship

Asteroid

You can give the sprites other names if you like, such as 'Asteroid Megadeath', or 'Jeremy'.

2 For this game, the spaceship needs to point to the right. Click on the spaceship in the **sprite area** and set the direction using the spinner in the **sprite menu.** (If the spaceship was drawn pointing up, the direction will be 180°.)

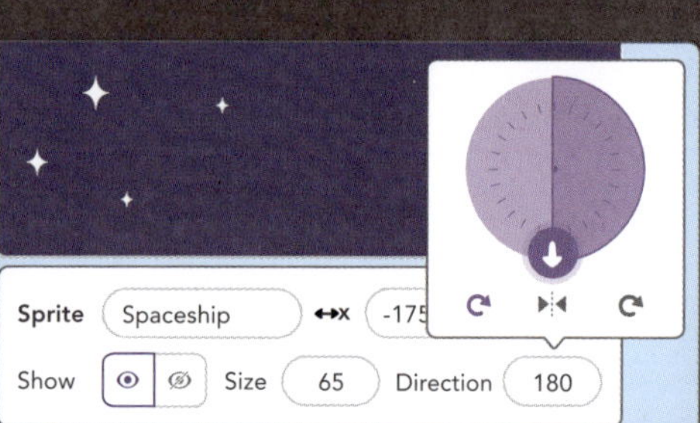

3 To make the spaceship smaller, find 'size' on the **sprite menu** and type in a smaller number.

Size 65

4 Open the **Backdrop Library** and add the backdrop 'Stars', or use one from the Usborne pack.

INFINITE SCROLLER

This game makes an endless stream of obstacles fly across the screen. The object is to move your spaceship up and down, using the mouse, to avoid them. This type of game is called an 'infinite scroller'. It goes on and on until you make a mistake.

Coding the spaceship

1 Select the spaceship in the **sprite area.** Make it go to the left side of the stage when the green flag is clicked.

```
when [green flag] clicked
set x to (-160)
```

-160 is almost the left-hand edge of the stage.

2 To move the spaceship up and down (changing its y coordinate) with the mouse, take a **set y to** block (from **Motion**) and add a **mouse y** variable (from **Sensing**).

```
set y to (mouse y)
```

3 Take a **repeat until** block (from **Control**) and add a **touching** block (from **Sensing**). Wrap this loop around the block from step 2.

```
touching [ ▾] ?

repeat until <touching [Asteroid ▾] ?>
    set y to (mouse y)
```

Select 'Asteroid' from the drop-down menu.

4 Now if you click the green flag, you can move the spaceship up and down with your mouse – but only until it crashes into an asteroid.

```
when [green flag] clicked
set x to (-160)
repeat until <touching [Asteroid ▾] ?>
    set y to (mouse y)
```

Coding the asteroid

1 Select the asteroid sprite and start a new script with a **green flag** (from **Events**).

2 Add a **go to** block (from **Motion**) to make the asteroid appear on the right of the stage.

Enter 240 (the right-hand edge of the stage) as the x value.

3 Add a **change x** block (from **Motion**) and enter a minus number. This will make the asteroid move left.

4 The asteroid should keep moving until the spaceship hits it. Wrap a **repeat until** loop around the **change x**, and set the condition with **touching** (from **Sensing**).

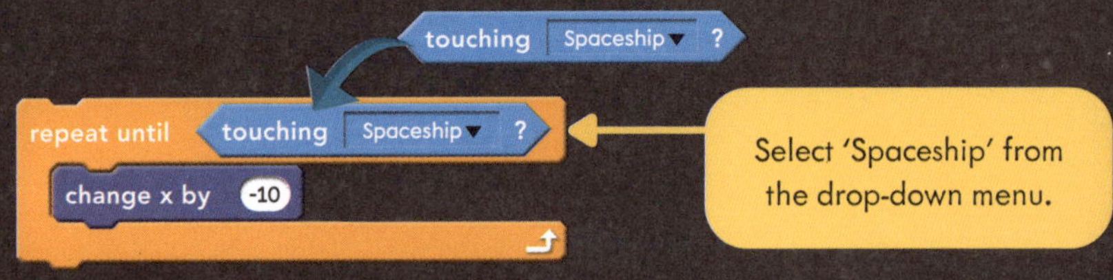

5 You also need to watch for the asteroid reaching the edge of the stage. Take a **less than** block (from **Operators**) and snap in **x position** (from **Motion**).

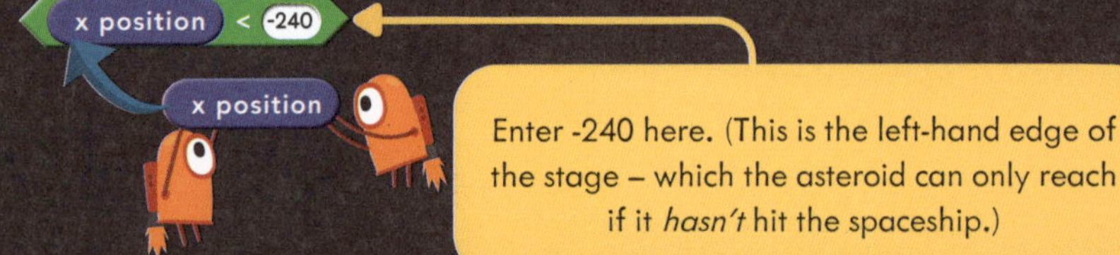

6 Snap this combined block into an **if/then** block (from **Control**).

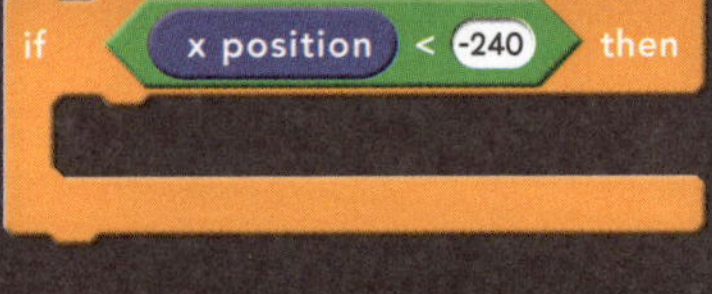

7 Insert a **set x** block inside, and enter 240 to send the asteroid back to the right-hand edge of the stage.

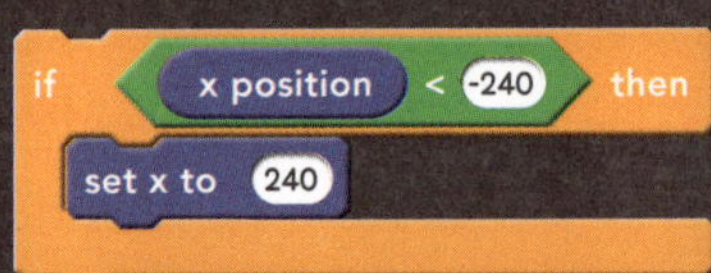

8 Add a **set y** block (from **Motion**) beneath the **set x** block. This decides the asteroid's height. Snap in **pick random** (from **Operators**) and enter 180 to -180, so it appears in a different place each time.

9 Insert the whole **if/then** stack into the **repeat until** loop from step 4. The final script should look like this.

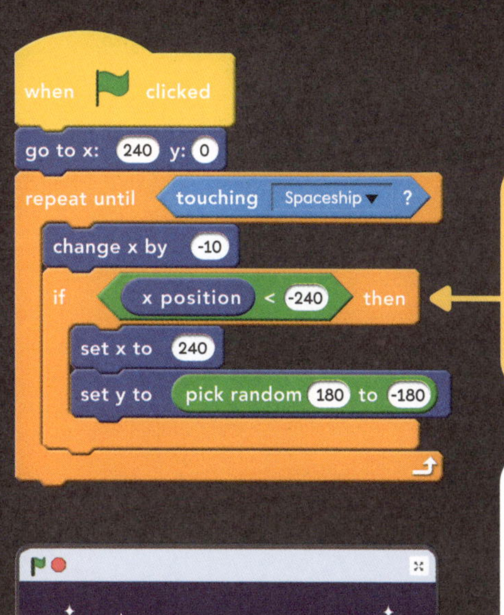

Now, every time the asteroid reaches the left of the stage, it will reappear on the right, as though it's a new asteroid altogether.

Try the game. It should seem as if you're zooming through an asteroid belt (although it's really one asteroid that keeps moving).

For a finishing touch, you can use variables to make the asteroids speed up, and count how many you dodge.

Speeding up

1 Go to the **Variables** menu and create a new variable called 'speed' – but this time, select 'For this sprite only'.

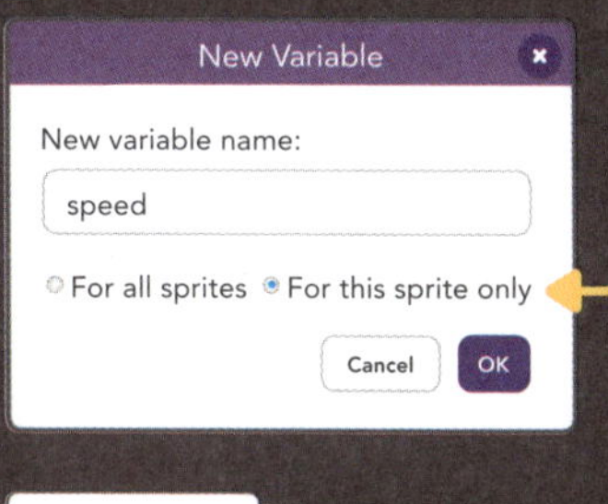

'For this sprite only' means the new variable blocks can only be used with *this* sprite.

2 Uncheck the box so the speed won't appear on the stage.

3 Select the asteroid sprite. To set its starting speed, insert a **set speed** block (from **Variables**) at the beginning of its script, like this.

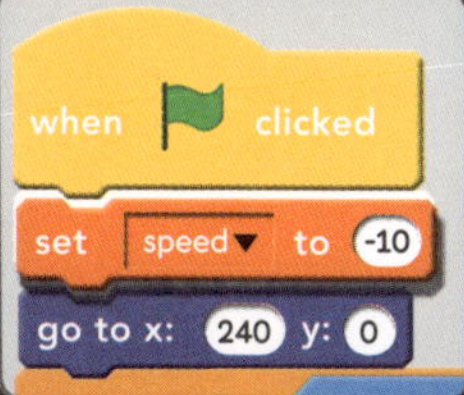

Set the starting speed to -10.

4 Now take a **speed** variable (from **Variables**) and snap it into the **change x by** block in the script.

```
change x by (speed)
```

This variable replaces the number '-10'.

5 To make the speed change during the game, insert a **change speed** block (from **Variables**) into the **if/then** stack, like this. Enter -1 to make it move left faster.

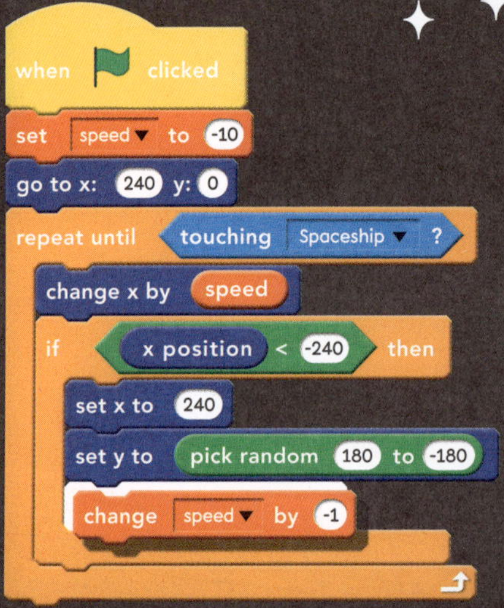

```
when [flag] clicked
set [speed] to (-10)
go to x: (240) y: (0)
repeat until <touching [Spaceship] ?>
    change x by (speed)
    if <(x position) < (-240)> then
        set x to (240)
        set y to (pick random (180) to (-180))
        change [speed] by (-1)
```

Try the game again. You should find each time an asteroid appears, it moves slightly faster. Soon, they will zip by – making them harder to dodge.

Keeping score

1 Go to the **Variables** menu and create a new **variable** called 'score'. This time, select 'For all sprites' and leave the box checked, so you can see the score on stage.

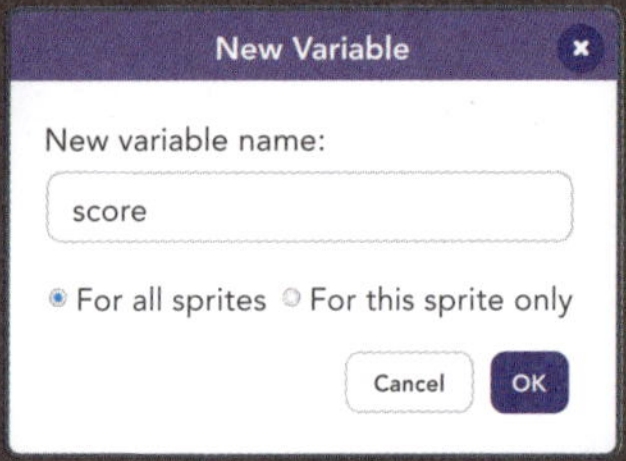

New Variable

New variable name:

score

For all sprites   For this sprite only

Cancel   OK

2 Select the asteroid sprite. Insert a **set score** block (from **Variables**) at the beginning, to make the score start from 0. Add a **change score** block at the bottom of the **if/then** stack, so the score goes up each time the asteroid resets.

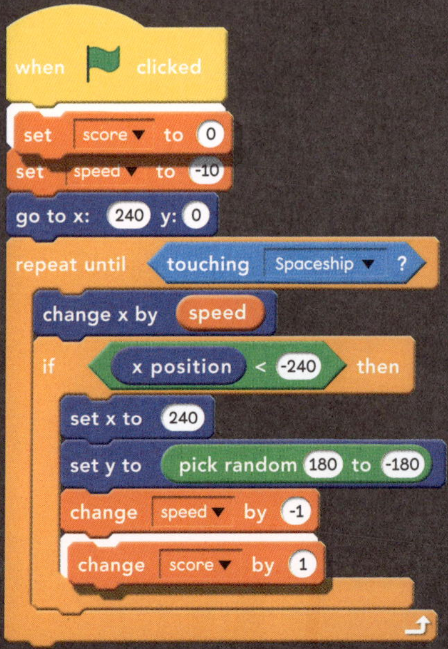

```
when [flag] clicked
set [score] to (0)
set [speed] to (-10)
go to x: (240) y: (0)
repeat until <touching [Spaceship] ?>
    change x by (speed)
    if <(x position) < (-240)> then
        set x to (240)
        set y to (pick random (180) to (-180))
        change [speed] by (-1)
        change [score] by (1)
```

To mix things up, you could add more obstacles – shooting stars, flying hippos... the choice is yours.

Find out how on the next page.

Speeding alien

1 Select a new 'Alien UFO' sprite and give it the same code as the asteroid.

2 Create *another* 'speed' variable and select 'For this sprite only', so it won't clash with the 'speed' you made before. Now the 'speed' in the alien code will refer to the *alien's* speed.

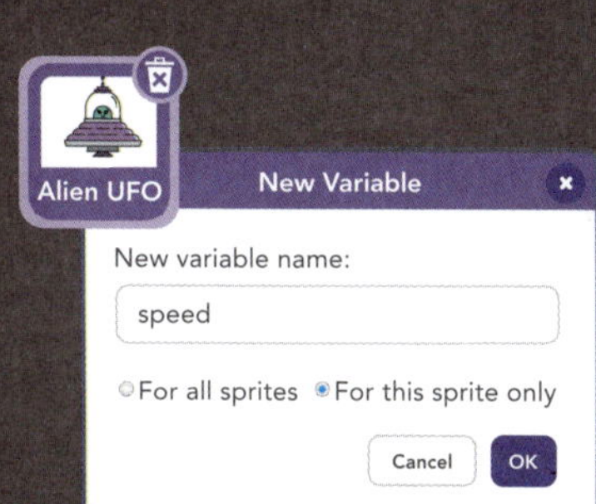

COPYING CODE

You can copy code between sprites using the BACKPACK at the bottom of the screen. Just click on the Backpack bar, drag in your script, switch sprites and drag it out again.

3 To reward yourself for dodging a speeding alien, enter a higher value in the **change score by** block.

4 Go to the script for the spaceship. Make it react to hitting an alien by adding an **or** (from **Operators**) plus another **touching** block, like this.

Add a **stop all** block to stop *all* the sprites (not just the one you hit) if you crash.

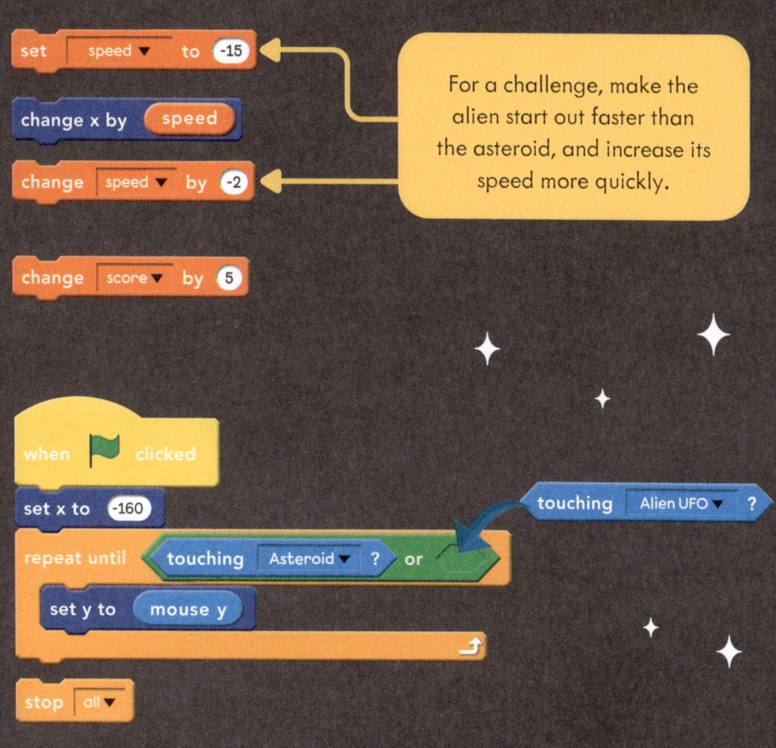

Play against your friends and see who can get the highest score!

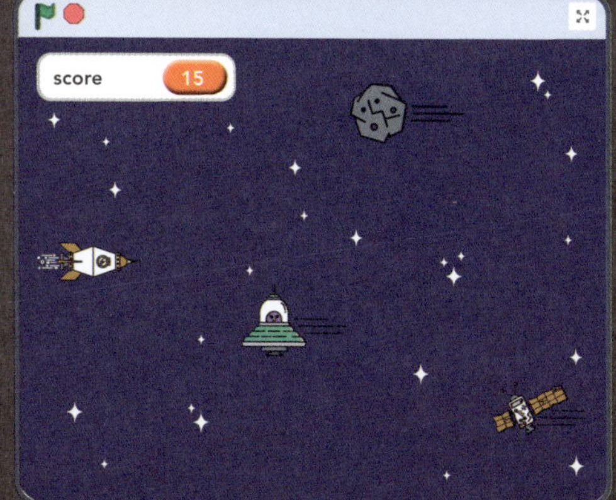

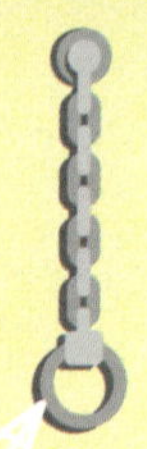

Jump

In this game, you help your hero to reach a distant door by leaping from ledge to ledge.

How to play

You control your hero using the arrow keys. Use the left and right arrows to run left or right, and the up arrow to jump.

The backdrop is made up of ledges you can jump between. The object is to reach the door without falling.

Find out how to choose a sprite and create your own backdrops, or access the starter pack (with a castle theme) at **usborne.com/Quicklinks**

Choose a hero

1 Start a new project, delete the cat and choose a new sprite. Click 'size' on the sprite menu and reduce the number to shrink your sprite.

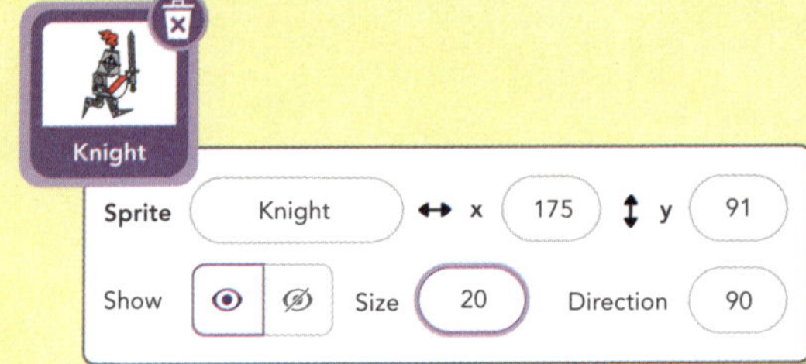

The sprite needs to be small, or the game will be too easy. We used 'Knight' and changed the size to '20'.

Build the ledges

2 To create a new backdrop, hover the mouse over the **Backdrop** button and select the **Paint** option.

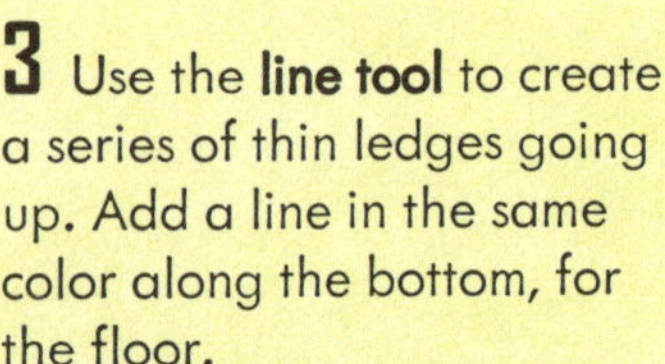

3 Use the **line tool** to create a series of thin ledges going up. Add a line in the same color along the bottom, for the floor.

On the highest ledge, in a new color, add the door you will be trying to reach.

COLOR MEANINGS

Each color needs to represent one thing.

We used:

Black = solid ground

Blue = door

Make sure you space out the ledges so the sprite needs to jump!

Coding your hero

You'll need three variables to keep track of whether the sprite is on solid ground or not, and how fast it is running and jumping.

1 Go to the **Variables** menu and create three variables. You could call them 'run speed', 'jump speed' and 'on ground?'. (Keep 'For all sprites' checked.)

run speed
jump speed
on ground?

Uncheck the boxes so the variables don't appear on the stage.

2 Take a **green flag** block (from **Events**) and three **set variable** blocks (from **Variables**). Add a **go to x y** block (from **Motion**). This ensures the sprite always begins standing in the right place.

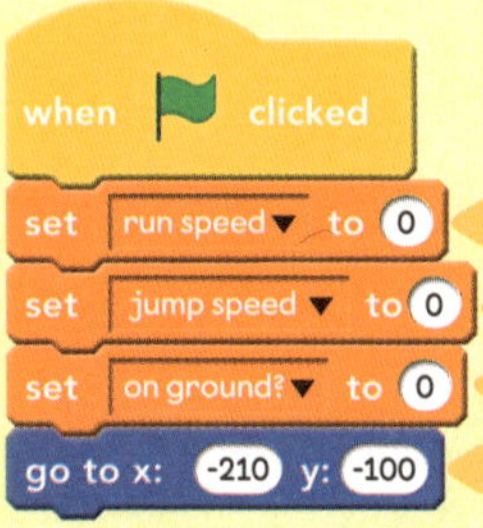

```
when [green flag] clicked
set [run speed] to (0)
set [jump speed] to (0)
set [on ground?] to (0)
go to x: (-210) y: (-100)
```

Select each variable from the drop-down menus, and enter '0' in the white boxes.

These values send the sprite to the bottom left-hand corner of the stage.

3 Now, you need a loop which runs until the sprite reaches the door. Take a **repeat until** (from **Control**) and snap in **touching color** (from **Sensing**). Add this below the script from step 2.

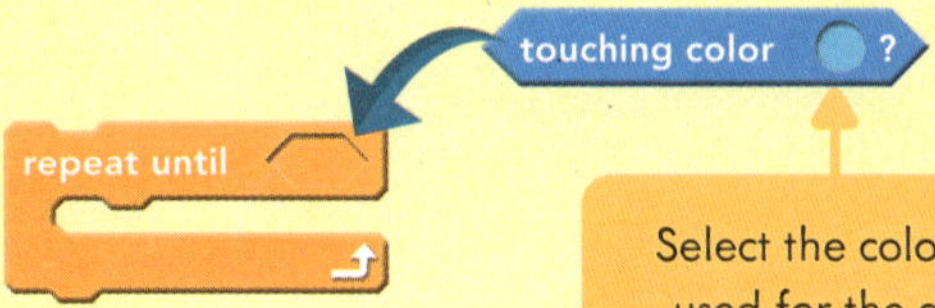

```
repeat until < touching color [ ] ? >
```

Select the color you used for the door.

4 To make the sprite move according to its speed, insert two **Motion** blocks into the loop: **change x by** and **change y by.** Then snap in **run speed** and **jump speed** variables (from **Variables**).

```
change x by (run speed)
change y by (jump speed)
```

x controls the sprite's left-right position, y its up-down position.

Falling

5 To make the sprite fall back after a jump, insert a **change variable** block (from **Variables**), select 'jump speed' and enter -1.

```
change [jump speed] by (-1)
```

A minus number will reduce the jump speed.

But when it hits solid ground, it should *stop* falling...

Hitting solid ground

6 Take an **if/then** block (from **Control**) and snap in an **and** (from **Operators**). Set the condition with a **touching color** block on one side, so the sprite reacts to the ground. On the other, put a **less than** block and add **jump speed.** Insert the finished **if/then** block inside the **repeat until** loop from step 3.

7 Insert another **repeat until** loop inside the **if/then** block from step 6. Make it repeat until the sprite is **not** touching the ground color. Insert a **change y by** in the middle.

8 Immediately below the **repeat until** loop (*inside* the **if/then** block), add two **set variable** blocks to update the values, so the sprite comes to rest on the ground. (Turn to page 70 if you want to see the whole script.)

Now you need to make it react to the keys...

Jumping

The sprite should jump only if the up arrow is pressed AND it is on the ground.

9 Take an **and** block. Snap in **key pressed** (from **Sensing**) on one side. On the other, add **on ground?** / **equals** and type in '1'.

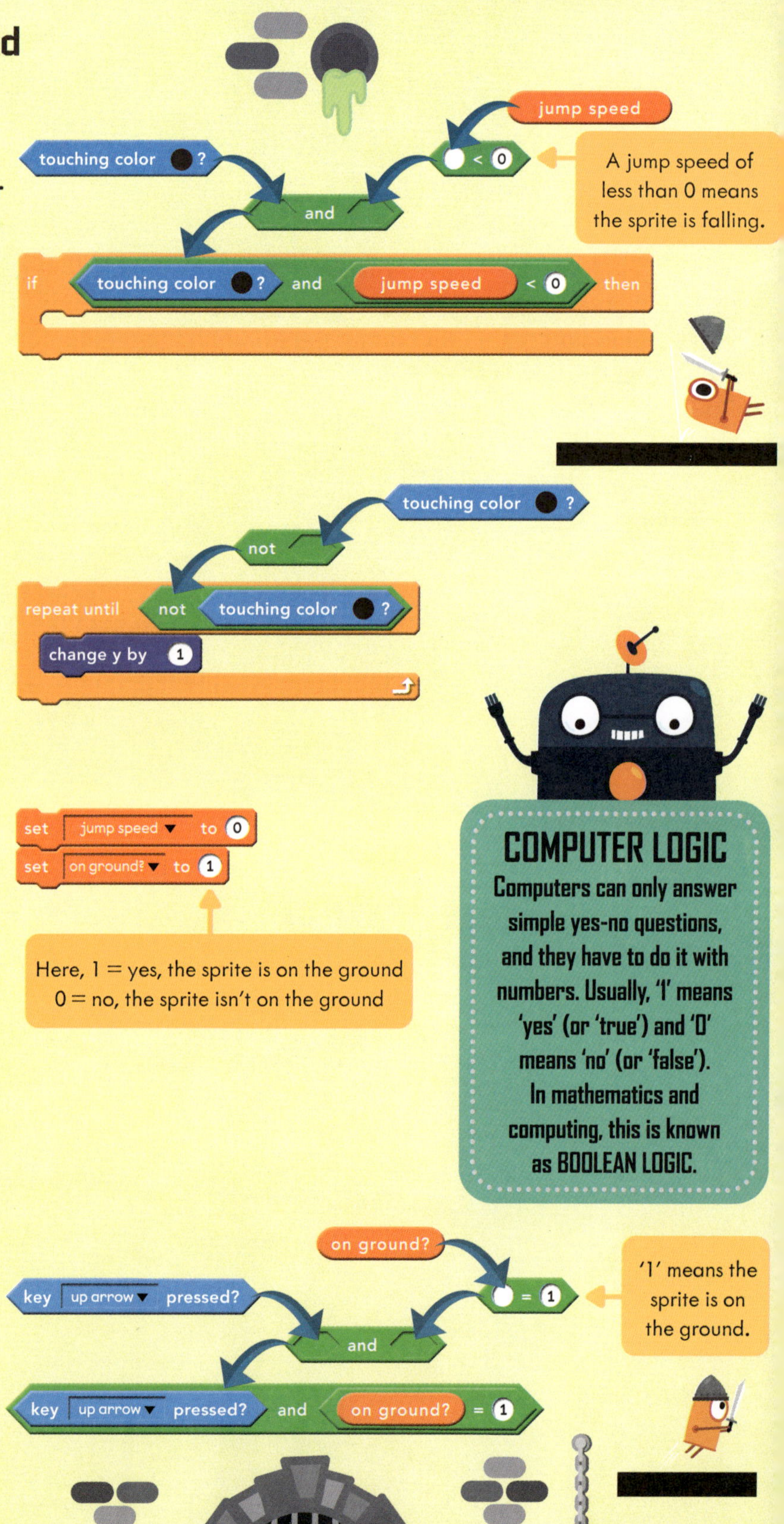

COMPUTER LOGIC

Computers can only answer simple yes-no questions, and they have to do it with numbers. Usually, '1' means 'yes' (or 'true') and '0' means 'no' (or 'false'). In mathematics and computing, this is known as BOOLEAN LOGIC.

10 Snap the whole thing into another **if/then** block. Then update your variables by inserting two **set variable** blocks (from **Variables**). Insert the whole stack inside the **repeat until** loop from step 3.

Running

To run, the sprite needs to react to the **left** and **right** arrow keys.

11 For the *left* arrow, take another **if/then** block and snap in **key pressed.** Insert a **change variable** block, select 'run speed' and enter a *minus* number.

12 For the *right* arrow, do the same but select 'right arrow' and enter a *plus* number.

Insert both these **if/then** stacks after the stack from step 10 (still inside the **repeat until** loop from step 3).

13 To make the sprite slow down if *no* key is pressed, take a **set variable** block and select 'run speed'. Set this to what you get when you **multiply** the **run speed** by *less than one.*

Insert this directly below the **if/then** stack from step 12 (still inside the **repeat until** loop from step 3).

Finishing

14 To finish, you could add a **start sound** block at the end of your script.

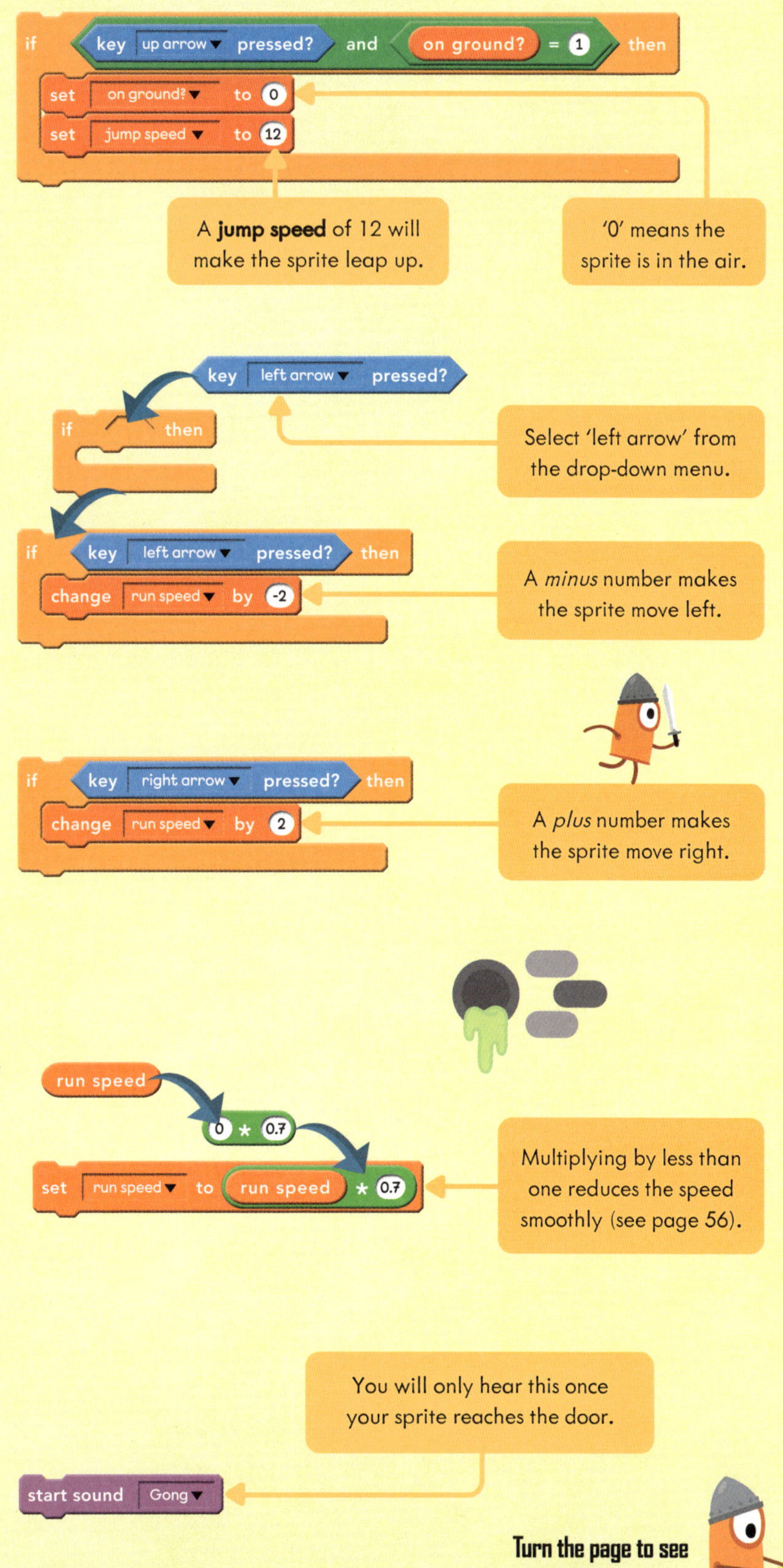

Turn the page to see the whole script.

Trying it out

This is what your finished code should look like... Click on the **green flag** to try it. (If it doesn't run, check carefully to make sure you've got all the right blocks, in the right order.)

Play a few times. Can you make your hero reach the door? Do you notice any problems?

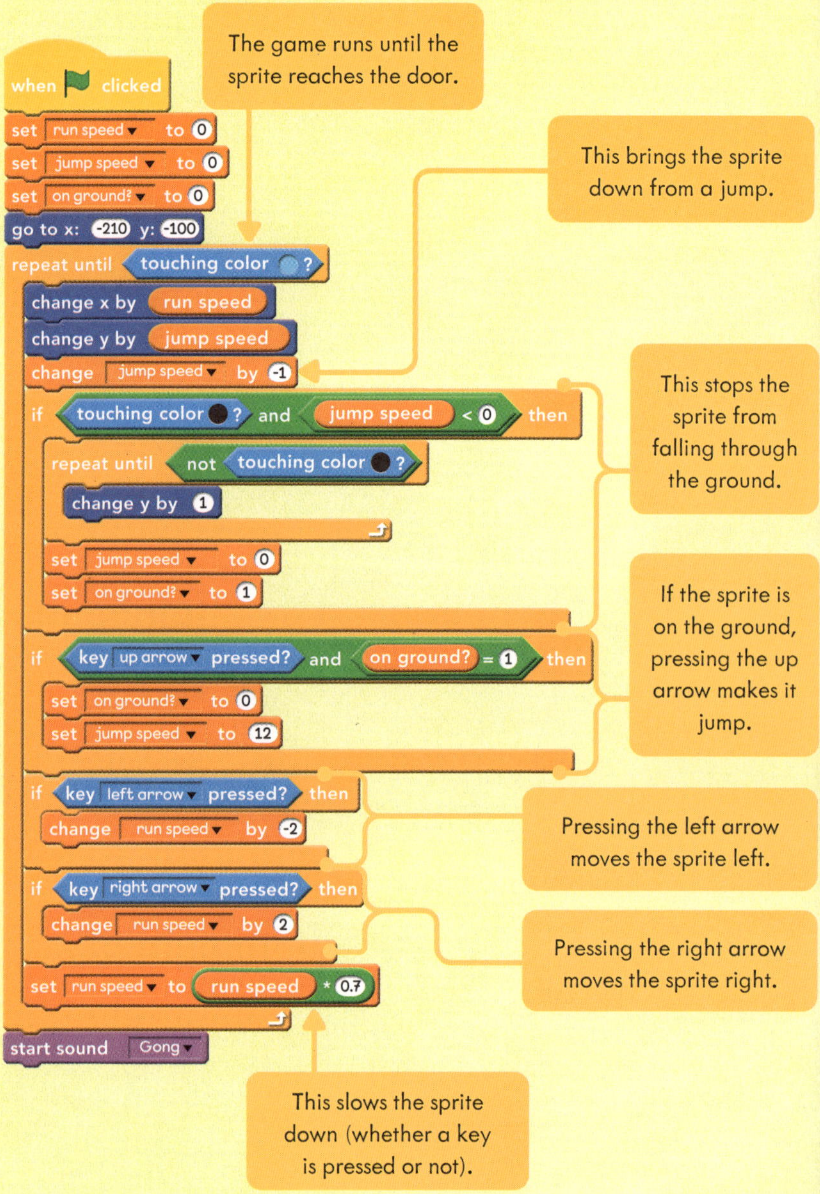

```
when [flag] clicked
set [run speed] to (0)
set [jump speed] to (0)
set [on ground?] to (0)
go to x: (-210) y: (-100)
repeat until <touching color [ ] ?>
    change x by (run speed)
    change y by (jump speed)
    change [jump speed] by (-1)
    if <<touching color [ ] ?> and <(jump speed) < (0)>> then
        repeat until <not <touching color [ ] ?>>
            change y by (1)
        end
        set [jump speed] to (0)
        set [on ground?] to (1)
    end
    if <<key [up arrow] pressed?> and <(on ground?) = (1)>> then
        set [on ground?] to (0)
        set [jump speed] to (12)
    end
    if <key [left arrow] pressed?> then
        change [run speed] by (-2)
    end
    if <key [right arrow] pressed?> then
        change [run speed] by (2)
    end
    set [run speed] to ((run speed) * (0.7))
end
start sound [Gong]
```

The game runs until the sprite reaches the door.

This brings the sprite down from a jump.

This stops the sprite from falling through the ground.

If the sprite is on the ground, pressing the up arrow makes it jump.

Pressing the left arrow moves the sprite left.

Pressing the right arrow moves the sprite right.

This slows the sprite down (whether a key is pressed or not).

A sinking feeling...

Did you spot the sprite sinking into ledges before rising up again? That's because of a small bug in this section of code...

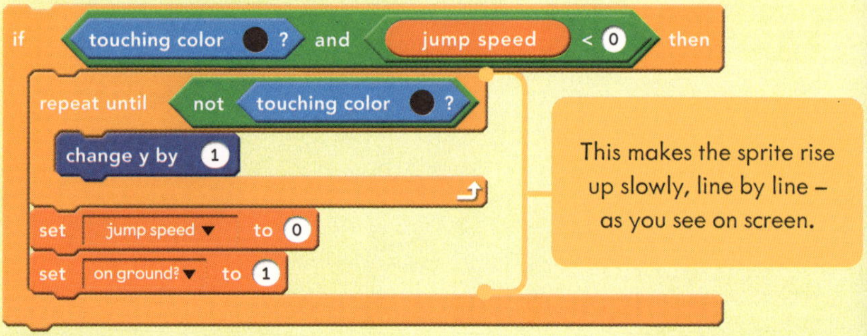

```
if <<touching color [ ] ?> and <(jump speed) < (0)>> then
    repeat until <not <touching color [ ] ?>>
        change y by (1)
    end
    set [jump speed] to (0)
    set [on ground?] to (1)
end
```

This makes the sprite rise up slowly, line by line – as you see on screen.

Fixing the bug

You can fix this using a new type of block, known as a **custom block.** This squashes a whole stack of blocks into one, helping to keep scripts neat and tidy. It also lets you run the stack faster.

1 Go to the **My Blocks** menu and click on **Make a Block.** Give the new block a name, such as **put on ground.** In Options, check 'Run without screen refresh'.

When you click 'OK', the new block will appear in the **My Blocks** menu.

2 A **define** block will also appear in the **script area.**

Separate the section of code which created the bug. Put it under the **define** block. This will make it run without showing on screen.

3 In the main script, insert a **put on ground** block to replace the blocks you removed.

Now try the game again. The sprite should react faster, without sinking visibly.

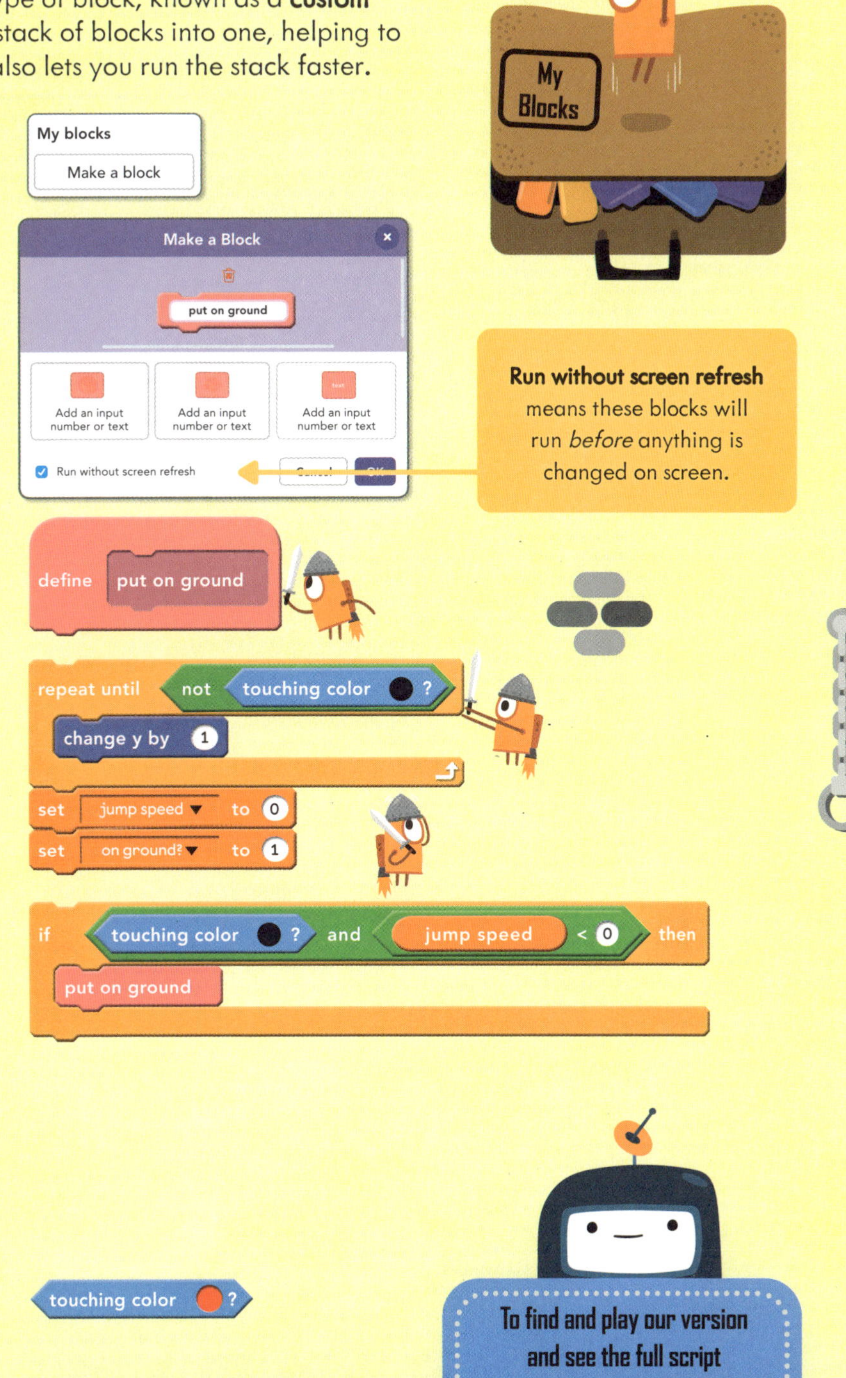

More game ideas

You could add booby traps in another color. If the sprite touches this color, send it back to the start.

You could also create more backdrops and add **switch backdrop,** so your hero has to climb more levels.

touching color ?

switch backdrop to next backdrop

To find and play our version and see the full script (including extras), go to usborne.com/Quicklinks

Balloon pop

In this game, you pop balloons by clicking on them. But beware the 'Doom' balloons – popping them will end the game.

Creating a start screen

1 Start a new project and delete the cat. Use the **painting tools** to create a backdrop and a new sprite made from text, or use the starter pack. We called the sprite 'start text' and included instructions on how to play.

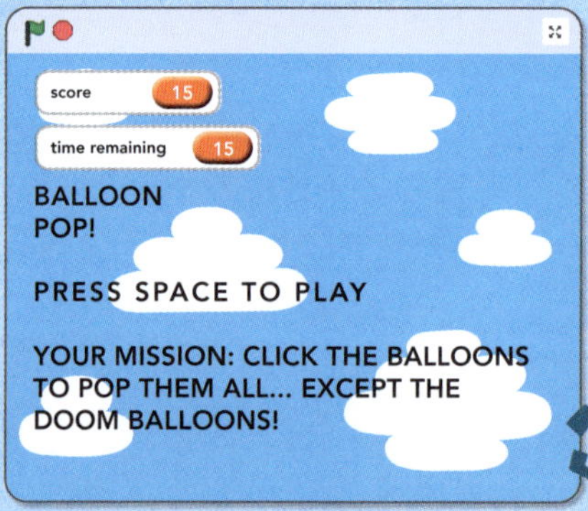

score 15
time remaining 15
BALLOON POP!
PRESS SPACE TO PLAY
YOUR MISSION: CLICK THE BALLOONS TO POP THEM ALL... EXCEPT THE DOOM BALLOONS!

Video games often use a title or start screen like this, to show the name of the game and any instructions.

2 With the 'start text' sprite selected, begin a script with a **green flag** and **broadcast**.

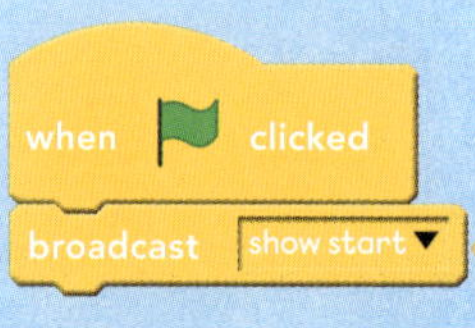

```
when green flag clicked
broadcast [show start ▼]
```

This broadcast will make the start screen appear.

3 Still on 'start text', begin a new script with **when I receive**, and add a **show** block to reveal the sprite. Then add **wait until** / **key space pressed** and **broadcast**, to make the game begin when you press the space bar. Finish with **hide**, to conceal the sprite again.

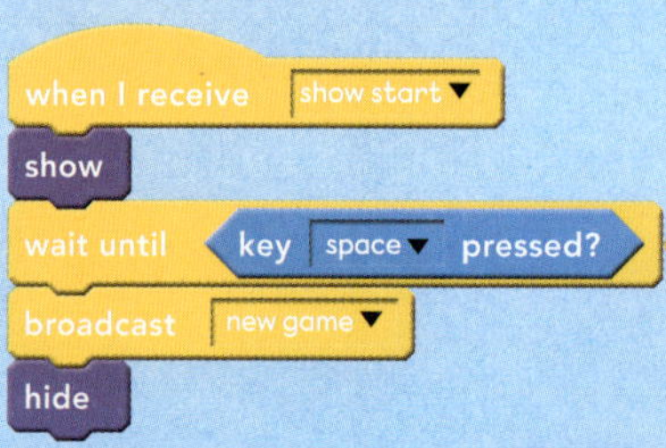

```
when I receive [show start ▼]
show
wait until <key [space ▼] pressed?>
broadcast [new game ▼]
hide
```

Select 'space' from the drop-down menu, to detect when the space bar is pressed.

The start screen is separate from the green flag, because it will be used again each time the game restarts.

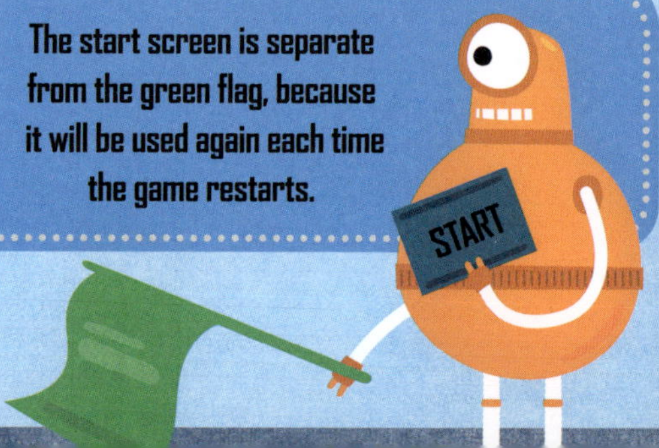

START

Coding the balloons

1 Add a balloon sprite from the Scratch library or Usborne pack. Make sure it's selected, then make a short script with **hide**, to conceal it while the start screen is showing.

2 Create two extra costumes for your balloon using the **painting tools**, or use the ones from the Usborne pack.

Time, speed and score

3 Start a new script for your balloon with **when I receive.**

Now to set up the scoring, control the balloon's speed and set a time limit. Go to **Variables** and create new variables for **score, speed** and **time remaining** (for all sprites). Then set their starting values, like this.

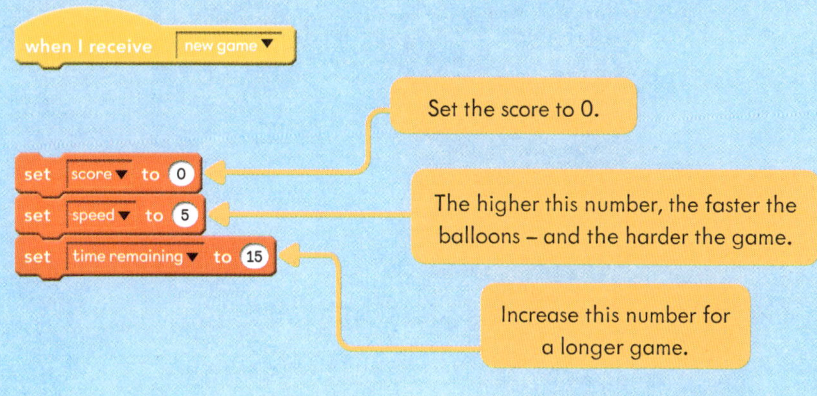

4 To make the game continue until you run out of time, add a **repeat until** loop. Make it finish when the **time remaining** equals 0, using the **Operators** block for **equals.**

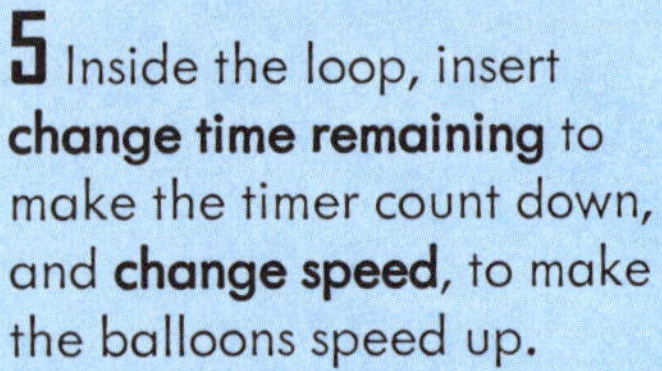

5 Inside the loop, insert **change time remaining** to make the timer count down, and **change speed**, to make the balloons speed up.

Then add **create clone**, to make more balloons, followed by a short **wait**.

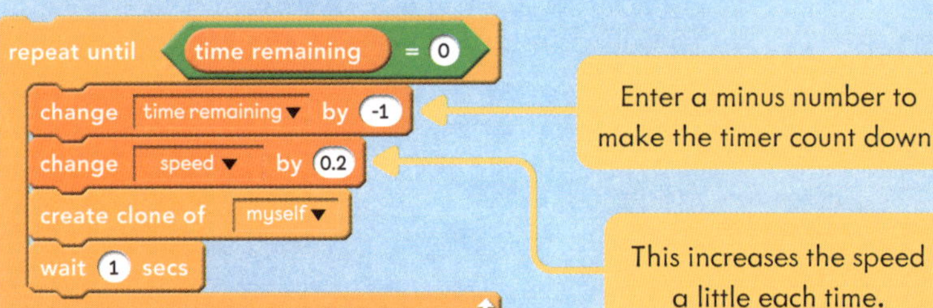

Enter a minus number to make the timer count down.

This increases the speed a little each time.

The loop repeats until the timer reaches zero. Make it count down in ones or halves, otherwise it could miss zero and never stop!

6 Below, choose a **sound** to finish the game, then **broadcast** a message to bring up a 'game over' screen (see page 77).

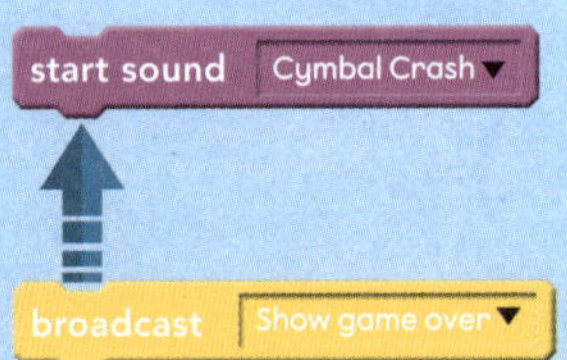

Clone controls

1 To control the clone balloons, start a new balloon script with **when I start as a clone** then **switch costume**. Pick a random number and use it to decide if the clone will be a 'Doom' balloon. If it is, use **switch costume** to change its appearance.

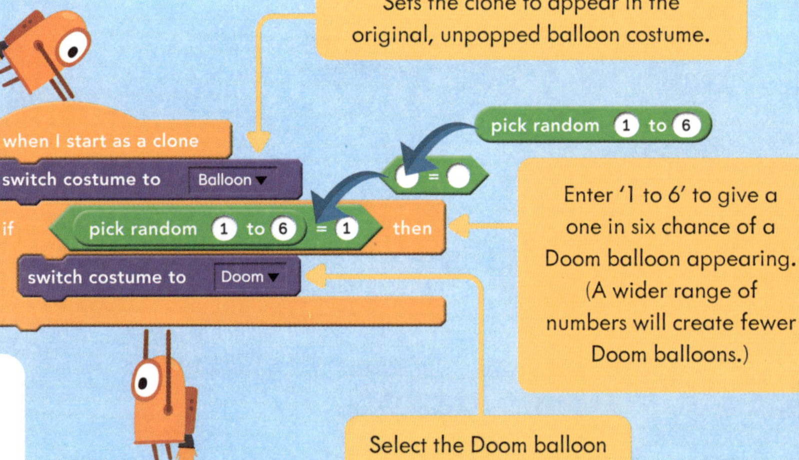

Sets the clone to appear in the original, unpopped balloon costume.

Enter '1 to 6' to give a one in six chance of a Doom balloon appearing. (A wider range of numbers will create fewer Doom balloons.)

Select the Doom balloon costume here.

2 Now make the clone balloon appear on stage. Use a **go to** block with a **random x** and a fixed **y**, so the clone can appear anywhere along the bottom.

3 To make the clone float upwards, you need to increase its **y** coordinate. Take a **repeat until** loop and insert **change y by** / **speed**. Make the loop run until the **y** value goes off the top of the screen. Then **delete this clone**.

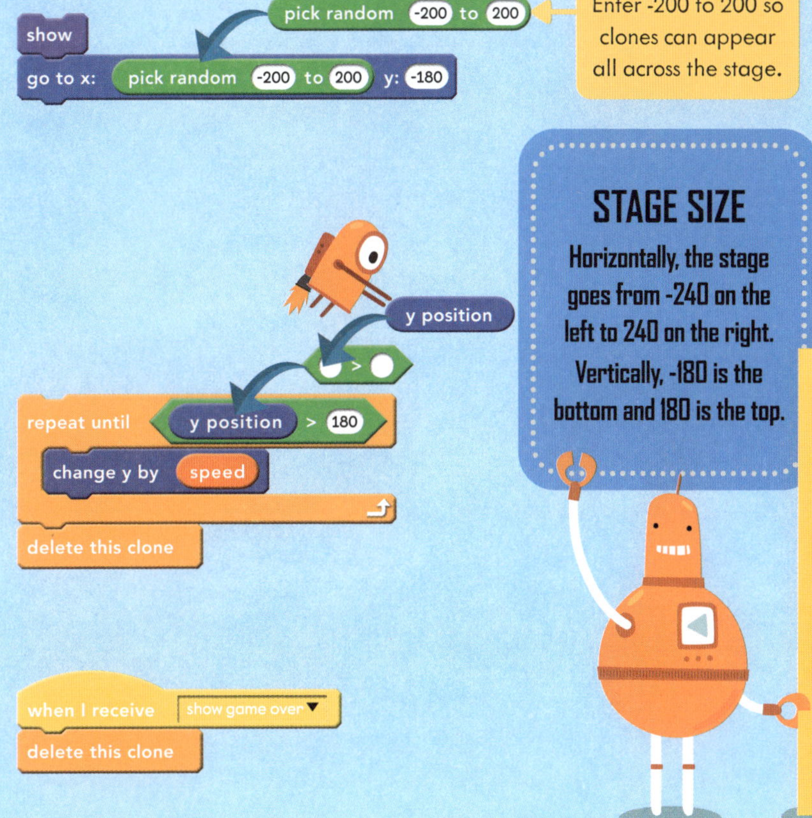

STAGE SIZE

Horizontally, the stage goes from -240 on the left to 240 on the right. Vertically, -180 is the bottom and 180 is the top.

4 To make sure there are no balloons left on stage at the end of the game, add a short script like this.

Pop goes the sprite

1 To pop the balloons, start a new script with **when this sprite clicked**.

What happens next depends on its costume, so take an **if/then** block and set the condition using **costume number** from **Looks**, like this.

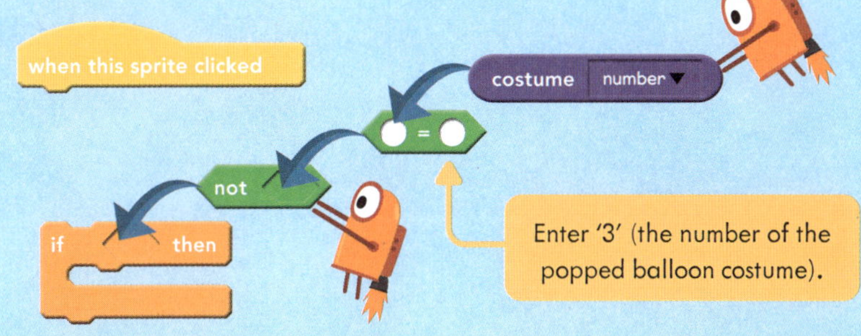

Underneath, insert a **stop**.

2 Now to spell out what happens for other costumes... Take an **if/else** block and set the condition using **costume number** again. Add this *inside* the **if/then** block from step 1.

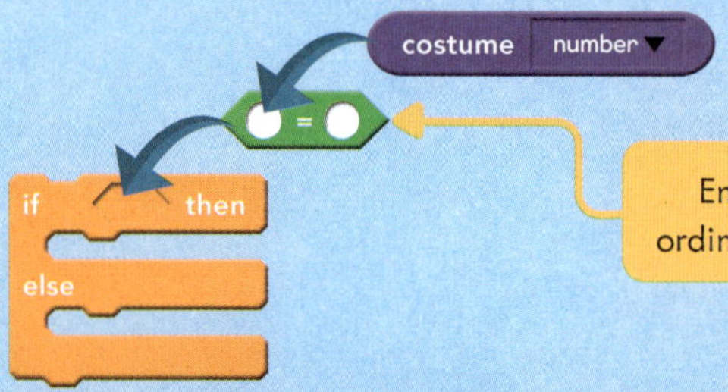

3 *If* it's an ordinary balloon, **start sound** 'pop' and increase the score. If it's not ordinary and it hasn't been popped, it must be... DOOM! In the **else** section, **start sound** (we chose a scream) and **set** the time remaining to 0.

4 Whichever balloon it was, it should now switch to the popped costume and then be deleted.

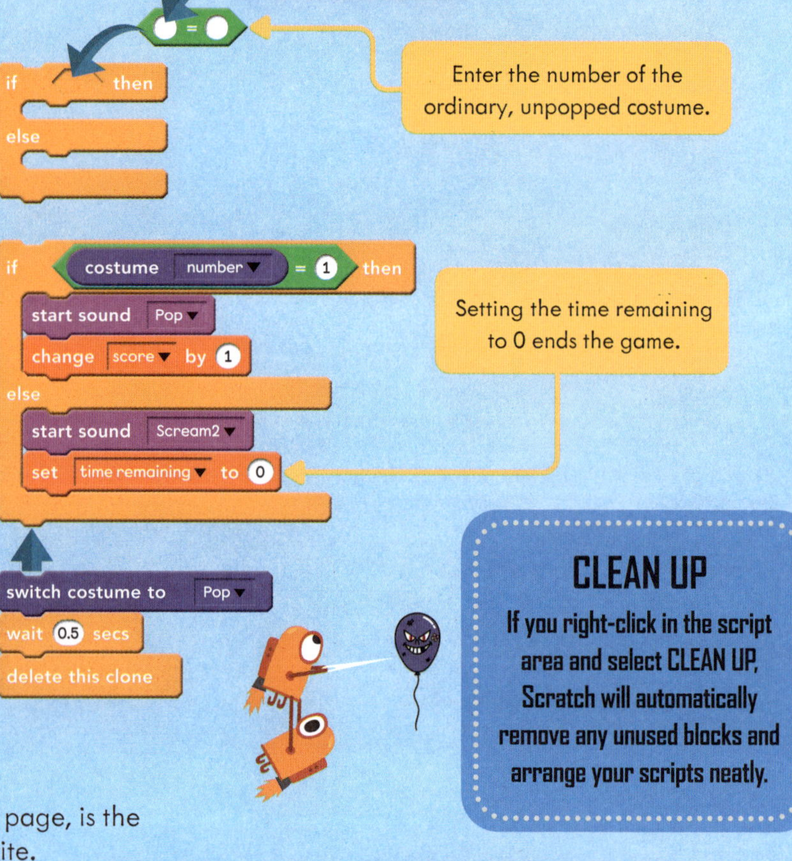

CLEAN UP

If you right-click in the script area and select CLEAN UP, Scratch will automatically remove any unused blocks and arrange your scripts neatly.

The finished code

Here, and on the top of the next page, is the finished code for the balloon sprite.

```
when [flag] clicked
hide
```

Hides the balloon while the start screen is showing.

```
when I receive [new game]
set [score] to (0)
set [speed] to (5)
set [time remaining] to (15)
repeat until <(time remaining) = (0)>
    change [time remaining] by (-1)
    change [speed] by (0.2)
    create clone of [myself]
    wait (1) secs
end
start sound [Cymbal Crash]
broadcast [Show game over]
```

These blocks reset score, speed and time remaining.

These blocks run down the timer, increase the speed and create clones.

This triggers the 'game over' screen.

```
when I receive [show game over]
delete this clone
```

This little script gets rid of any remaining balloons at the end of the game.

CLONE-O-MATIC

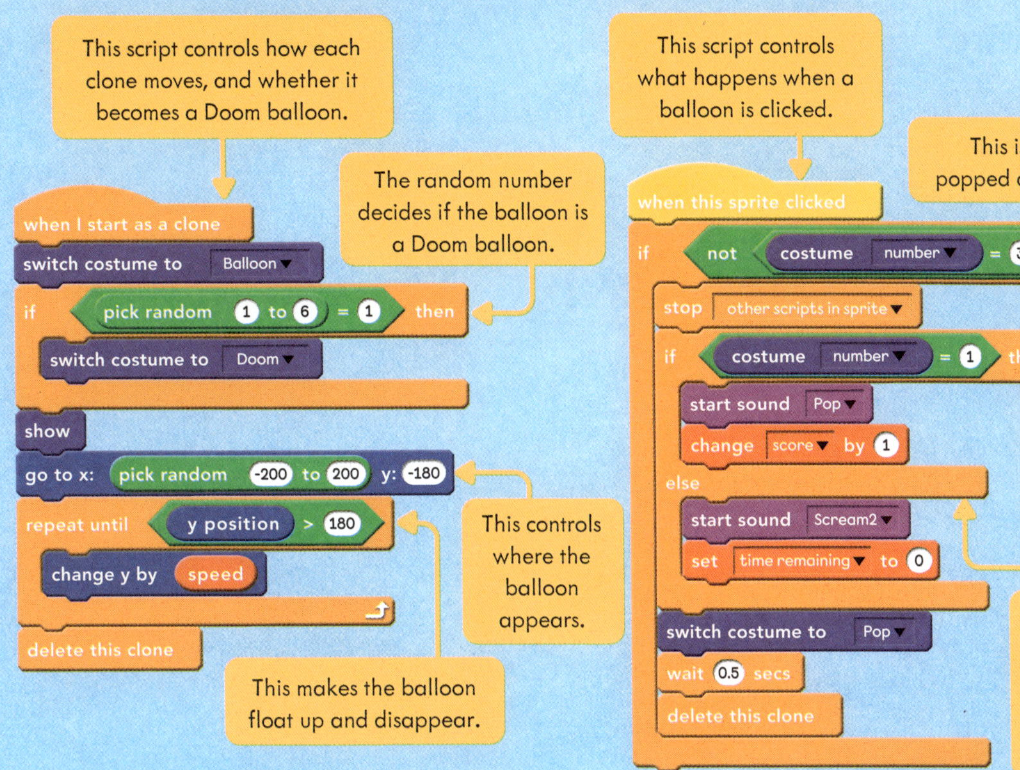

Game over

1 To add a 'game over' screen, you need to create another text sprite, like this, and hide it.

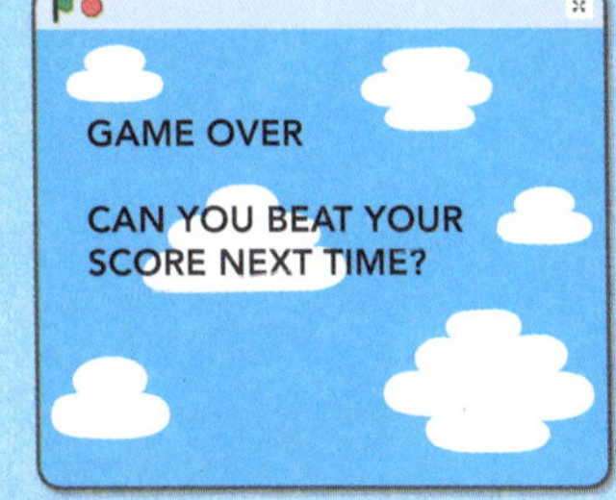

PLAYING

The game works best if you click on the FULL SCREEN BUTTON before playing.

Click on the RETURN BUTTON to return to your coding screen.

2 Then, give it a simple script to make it appear at the end, before hiding and calling up the start screen.

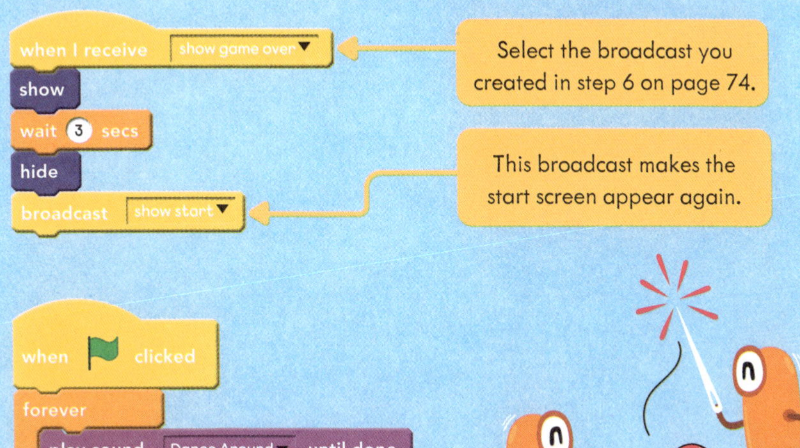

A soundtrack

3 If you'd like to give your game a soundtrack, select the **backdrop** and add a script like this. It will play during the start and game over screens, too.

broadcast
Giga 3

erase all
start sound
Meow
set size to
100
%

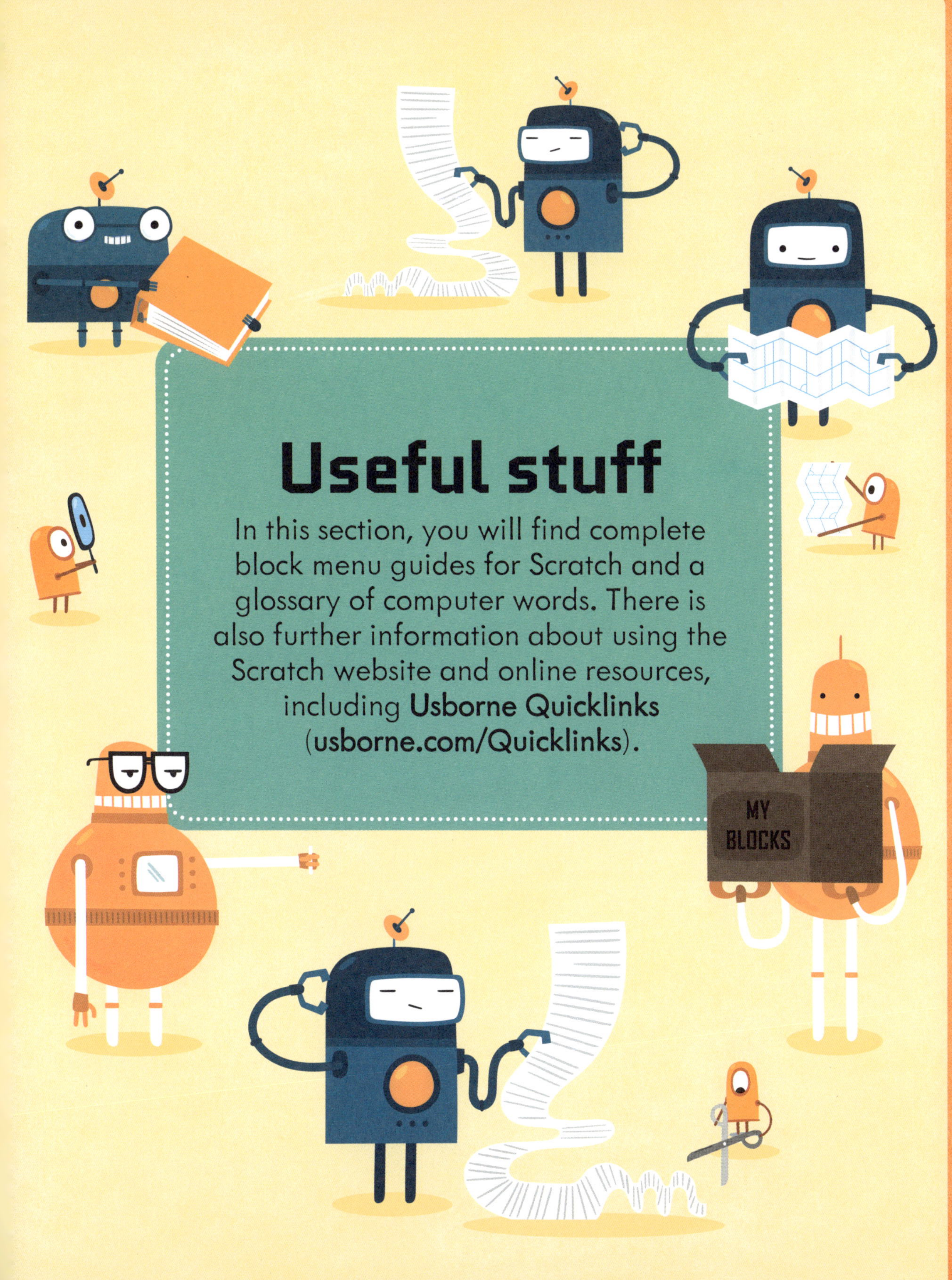

Useful stuff

In this section, you will find complete block menu guides for Scratch and a glossary of computer words. There is also further information about using the Scratch website and online resources, including **Usborne Quicklinks** (**usborne.com/Quicklinks**).

Saving and sharing

Scratch automatically saves what you do. But if you want to keep a project after closing it, you'll need to give it a name. If you are using Scratch online, you need a **Scratch account** to do this.

Setting up a Scratch account

You will need an adult's permission to set up an account.

1 Go to the Scratch website (you will find a link to it at **Usborne Quicklinks**). Click on **Join Scratch.**

2 Choose a **username** and **password**. Go through the steps and fill in the details, including an email address.

3 Scratch will send out an email. When it arrives, follow the instructions to confirm the account.

Once you have an account, you can click 'sign in' to get to it.

Naming and finding projects

1 When you start a new project, give it a name in the box above the stage. This will save it automatically into a folder called 'My Stuff'.

2 To see your saved projects, click on the 'S' folder in the top-right corner. Click on a project to open it.

Usborne account

You can see working versions of all the scripts in this book by going to the Usborne Scratch account. Go to **usborne.com/Quicklinks** for a link and full instructions.

UPDATES

The online version of Scratch is constantly being updated and added to, so it is possible that some details may change. If this happens, you will find updates at Usborne Quicklinks.

Sharing projects

When sharing, it's a good idea to add instructions on how your project works.

LEARNING MORE

Sharing your projects and looking at other people's is a great way to get feedback and learn more. The Scratch website makes it easy to share things with other Scratch users.

1 Click **See project page** and add your instructions, such as which keys to press.

2 Then, click the **Share** button. Now other people can try out your code.

To get back to the coding screen, click **See inside.**

See inside

Remixing

The Scratch site also lets you explore other people's projects and make your own versions, known as **remixing.**

1 Open any project and click **See inside** to see the code.

2 Change it or add your own ideas, then click **Remix.** The new version will be saved in your 'My Stuff' folder.

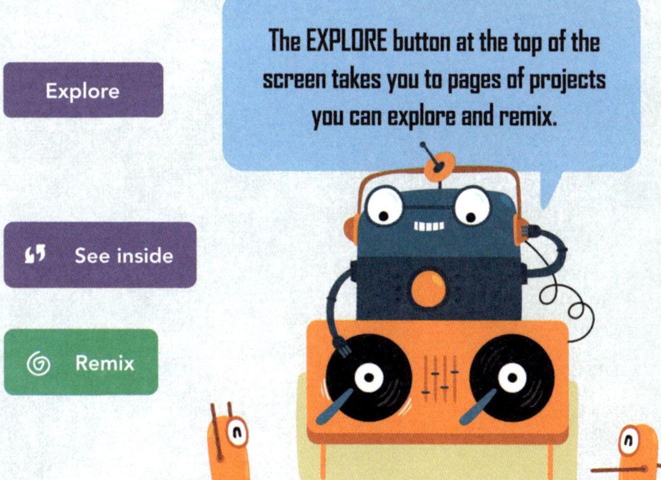

Backpack

The **Backpack** lets you store scripts, sprites and backdrops to use again later.

1 You'll find your Backpack at the bottom of the screen. Click on the bar to open it.

2 Drag scripts, sprites and backdrops into your Backpack to add them. (Right-click and delete to remove them.)

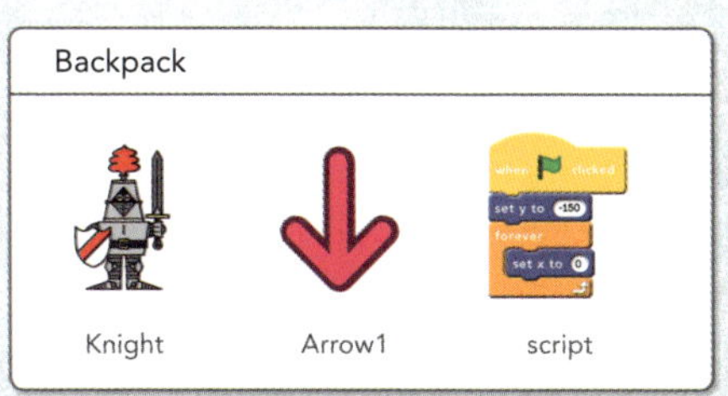

To use an item from your Backpack, just drag it out onto your project screen.

Menu guide

Here is a complete list of every block in every menu, and what it does.

MOTION

Motion blocks move sprites around the stage.

Ordinary instructions are in rectangular blocks, also known as **stack** blocks, because they can be stacked one on top of another.

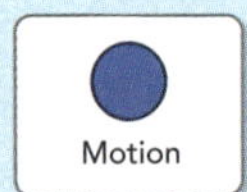

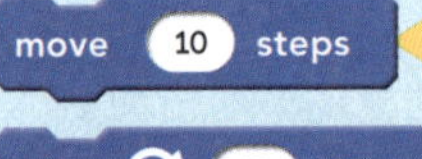

moves a sprite in the direction it is currently facing

turn ↻ 15 degrees — turns a sprite right

turns a sprite left

go to random position ▾ — sends a sprite to the same position as something else, e.g. the mouse-pointer (selected from the drop-down menu)

immediately sends a sprite to the given coordinates

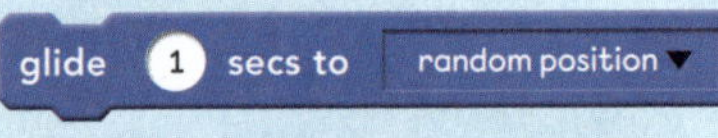

moves a sprite smoothly to something (selected from the drop-down menu)

glide 1 secs to x: 0 y: 0 — moves a sprite smoothly to the given coordinates, in the given time

points a sprite in a particular direction, given in degrees (90 degrees = right, -90 = left)

point towards mouse-pointer ▾ — points a sprite towards something (selected from the drop-down menu)

change x by 10 — changes a sprite's **x** or left-right coordinate (the value can range from 240 to -240)

set x to 0 — sets a sprite's **x** or left-right coordinate (0 puts it in the middle)

change y by 10 — changes a sprite's **y** or up-down coordinate (the value can range from 180 to -180)

set y to 0 — sets a sprite's **y** or up-down coordinate (0 puts it in the middle)

if on edge, bounce — sends the sprite back in the opposite direction when it reaches the edge of the stage

set rotation style left-right ▾ — decides if a sprite can turn around, flip upside down, or always face the same way

x position — lets you use a sprite's **x** position as a variable

y position — lets you use a sprite's **y** position as a variable

direction — lets you use a sprite's direction as a variable

LOOKS

Looks blocks control the appearance of sprites and backdrops, including speech bubbles and special effects.

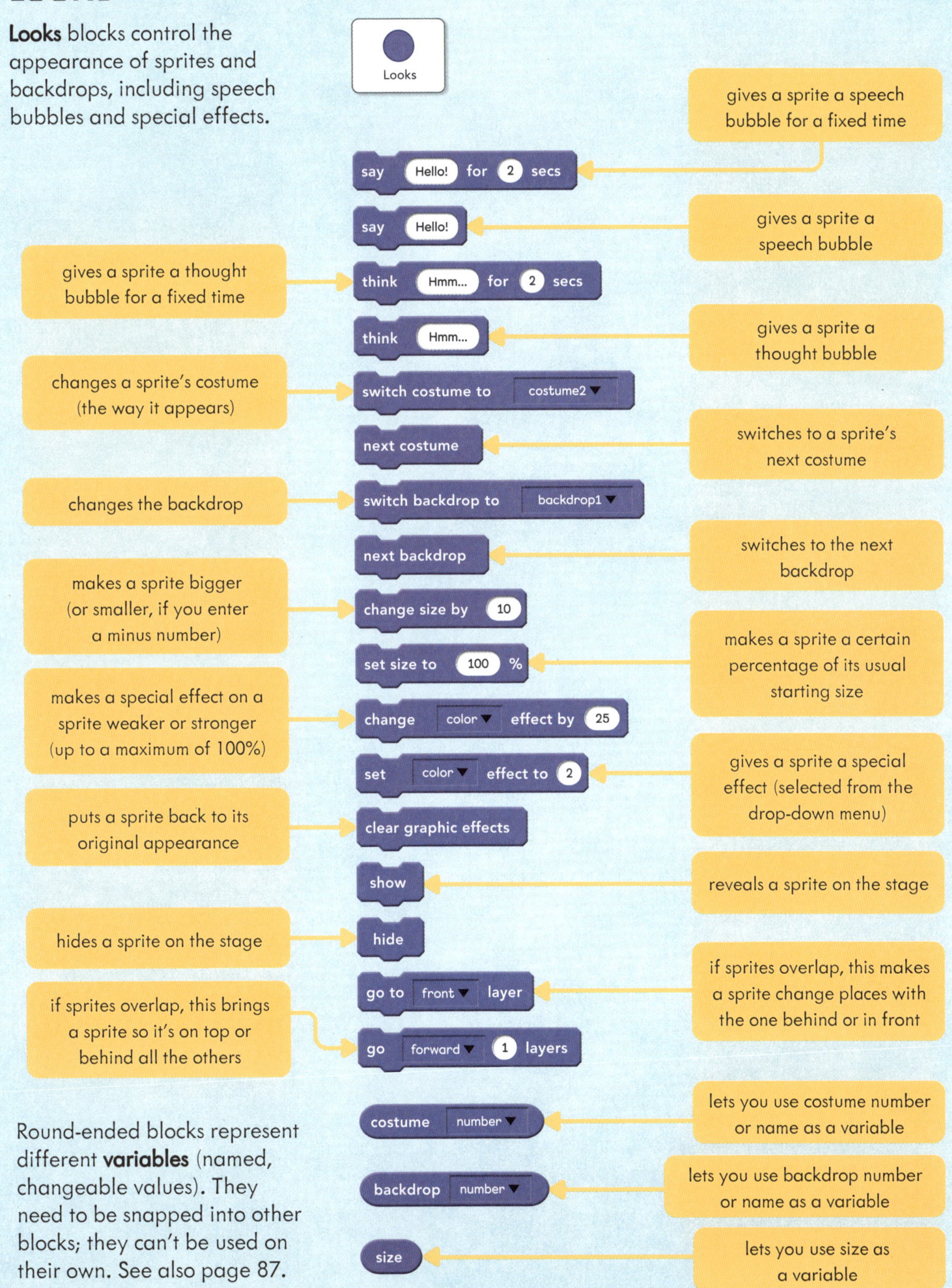

Round-ended blocks represent different **variables** (named, changeable values). They need to be snapped into other blocks; they can't be used on their own. See also page 87.

SOUND

Sound blocks control sounds. Scratch comes with a library of sounds you can use – just remember to add each sound from the library to your script first. You can also record your own sounds.

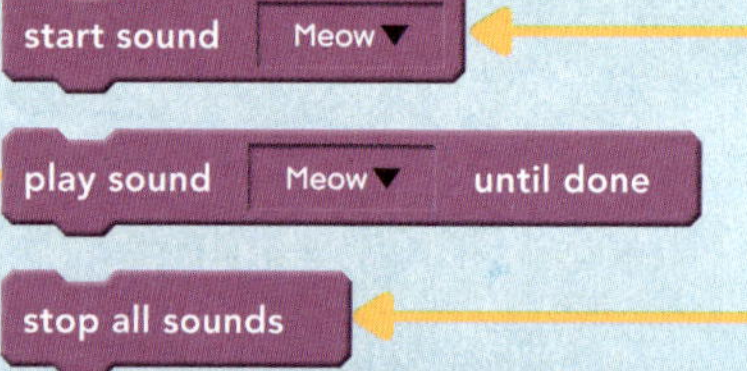

- **start sound Meow** – plays a sound (selected from the drop-down menu) once
- **play sound Meow until done** – plays a sound and waits until it is finished
- **stop all sounds** – stops any sounds that are playing
- **change pitch effect by 10** – makes a sound effect weaker or stronger (up to a maximum of 100%)
- **set pitch effect to 100** – Gives a sound a special effect (selected from the drop down menu)
- **clear sound effects** – Removes any sound effects
- **change volume by -10** – makes sounds louder (with a plus number) or quieter (with a minus number)
- **set volume to 100 %** – sets the volume
- **volume** – lets you use volume as a variable

MUSIC

Music blocks control music effects. You can add the **Music** menu to the block menu by using the **Extensions** button (see page 91).

- **play drum (1) Snare Drum for 0.5 beats** – plays one of a choice of drum sounds, for a certain number of beats
- **rest for 0.25 beats** – waits for a certain number of beats before continuing
- **play note 60 for 0.25 beats** – plays a note (given as a number) on the selected instrument, for a certain number of beats
- **set instrument to (1) Piano** – selects an instrument
- **set tempo to 60** – sets the speed or 'tempo'
- **change tempo by 20** – speeds up (with a plus number) or slows down (with a minus number) all notes
- **tempo** – lets you use tempo as a variable

EVENTS

Events blocks control when things happen.

Events

Hat-shaped blocks, with curved tops, are used to **start** scripts.

when [green flag] clicked — starts a script when the green flag above the stage is clicked

when [space ▼] key pressed — starts a script when a key is pressed (you select which key from the drop-down menu)

when this sprite clicked — starts a script when the sprite is clicked

when backdrop switches to [backdrop1 ▼] — starts a script when the backdrop changes

when [loudness ▼] > (10) — starts a script when the value of a variable changes (you select which variable from the drop-down menu)

when I receive [message1 ▼] — starts a script when a message is received from another part of the code

broadcast [message1 ▼] — sends a message to another part (or parts) of the code

broadcast [message1 ▼] and wait — sends a message to another part (or parts) of the code *and* waits for that code to run before continuing

ONLINE GUIDE

Scratch also has an online guide or WIKI where you can browse blocks by type and shape, as well as find other useful information.

Go to **usborne.com/Quicklinks** for a link.

CONTROL

Control blocks control the code itself, including when and how long it runs. You can also use control blocks to create 'clones' or exact duplicates of a sprite.

C-shaped blocks wrap around other instructions – often to create repeating **loops.**

Loops always have an up arrow at the end.

C-shaped **if/then/else** blocks set the conditions for other things to happen.

Cap blocks (blocks with a straight bottom) are used to **end** scripts.

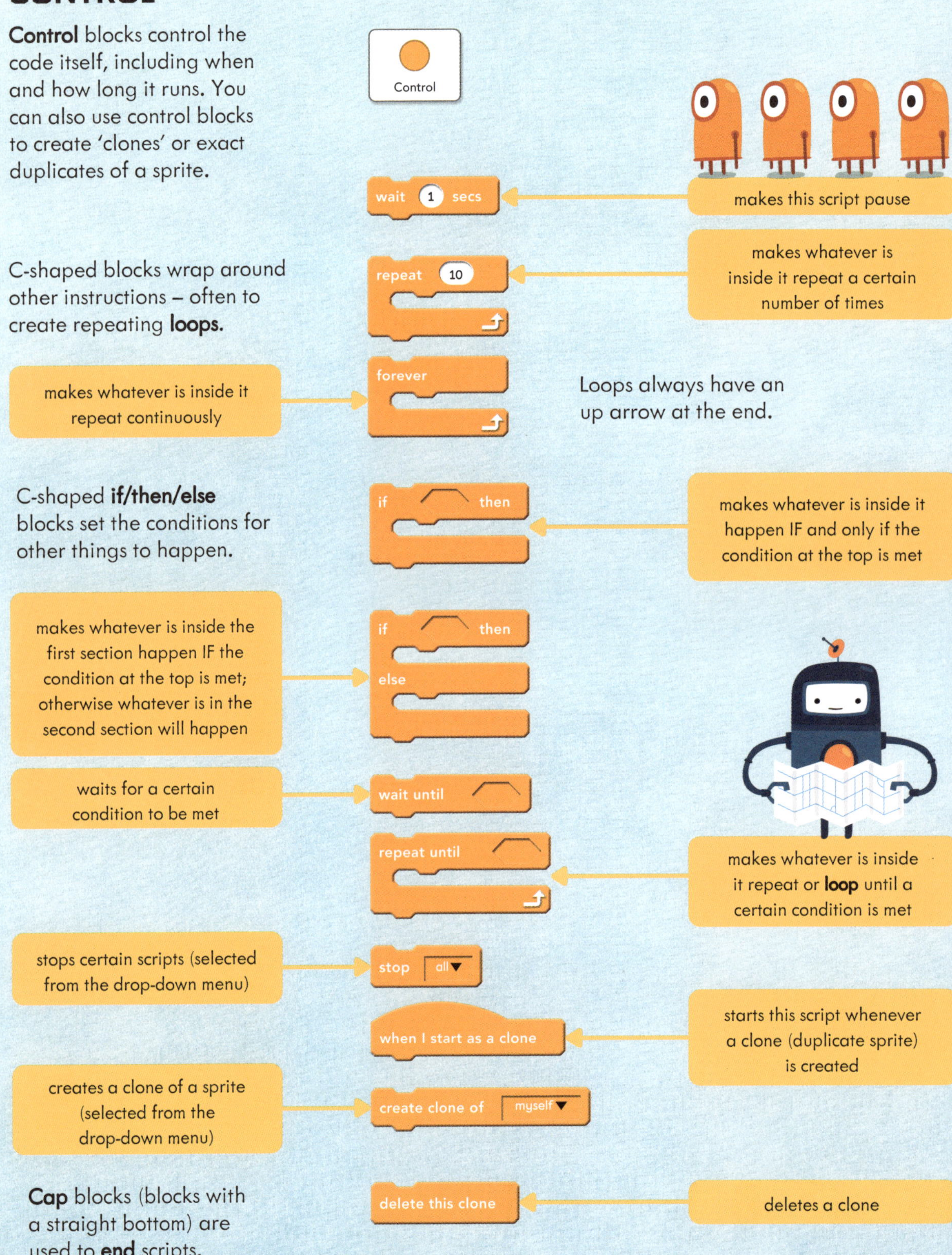
Control
wait 1 secs
makes this script pause
repeat 10
makes whatever is inside it repeat a certain number of times
forever
makes whatever is inside it repeat continuously
if then
makes whatever is inside it happen IF and only if the condition at the top is met
if then else
makes whatever is inside the first section happen IF the condition at the top is met; otherwise whatever is in the second section will happen
wait until
waits for a certain condition to be met
repeat until
makes whatever is inside it repeat or loop until a certain condition is met
stop all
stops certain scripts (selected from the drop-down menu)
when I start as a clone
starts this script whenever a clone (duplicate sprite) is created
create clone of myself
creates a clone of a sprite (selected from the drop-down menu)
delete this clone
deletes a clone

SENSING

Sensing blocks are used to set conditions for other blocks. Most of them are round- or diamond-ended, and need to be snapped into other blocks. These types of blocks can't be used on their own.

Diamond-ended blocks set **if conditions.** In Scratch, these are sometimes known as **Booleans**, because they use 'Boolean' or simple yes-no logic.

Round-ended blocks represent **variables.** In Scratch, these are also known as **reporters**, because they 'report back' on a particular condition.

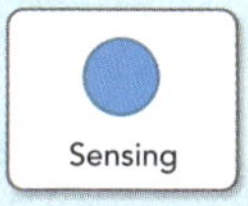

Sensing

touching mouse-pointer ▾ ?	checks if the sprite is touching something (selected from the drop-down menu)
touching color ?	checks if the sprite is touching a color (you set the color by clicking in the box and then on screen)
color is touching ?	checks if a particular color is touching another, specified color (you set the colors by clicking in the boxes and then on screen)
distance to mouse-pointer ▾	lets you use the distance to something (selected from the drop-down menu) as a variable
ask What's your name? and wait	makes a sprite ask a question
answer	lets you use the answer to a question as a variable
key space ▾ pressed?	checks if a particular key has been pressed (you select the key from the drop-down menu)
mouse down	checks whether a mouse button has been pressed
mouse x	lets you use the left-right position of the mouse as a variable
mouse y	lets you use the up-down position of the mouse as a variable
set drag mode draggable ▾	sets whether a sprite can be dragged or not
loudness	lets you use volume as a variable
timer	records how much time has passed and lets you use that as a variable
reset timer	makes the timer go back to 0
backdrop# ▾ of Stage ▾	lets you use information about the stage or a sprite as a variable.
current year ▾	lets you use the current date or time as a variable
days since 2000	counts the days since January 1st, 2000
username	lets you use a player's username as a variable IF they are logged in to the Scratch site

OPERATORS

Operators blocks are used to do math and set out conditions such as 'and', 'or' and 'not' (often known in coding as 'logic').

All **Operators** are round- or diamond-ended, and need to be snapped into other blocks.

These round-ended blocks (or **reporters**) allow you to do math with different variables.

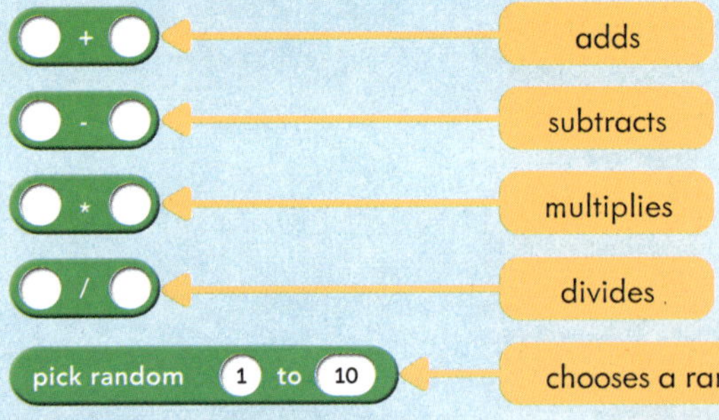

Diamond-ended blocks (or **Booleans**) set conditions.

numbers or variables go in the white boxes

> — checks if the first value is greater than the second

< — checks if the first value is less than the second

= — checks if two values are equal

these boxes must be completed by more diamond-ended blocks

and — checks if both conditions are true

or — checks if one or other or both conditions are true

not — checks if a condition is *not* true

join apple banana — joins two variables together

letter 1 of apple — takes a specified character from a word (here, letter 1 is 'a')

apple contains a ? — checks whether a piece of text contains a particular character

length of apple — counts the characters in a word

mod — records the remainder (the amount left over) after dividing the first value by the second

round — rounds an amount to the nearest whole number

abs ▼ of — used for advanced math, such as finding square roots or working out angles using trigonometry

VARIABLES

Variables blocks are for managing information – either as a single, named piece of information, known as a **variable**, or as a **list**.

To use **Variables** blocks, you first need to tell the computer to 'Make a Variable' OR 'Make a List'.

When you select 'Make a Variable', you will be asked to give it a name.* Then, a set of new blocks with that name will appear in the **Variables** menu.

Variables are used to manage numbers which might change, such as your speed or score in a game.

When you select 'Make a List', you will be asked to give the list a name. Then, a set of new blocks with that name will appear in the **Variables** menu.

Lists keep track of several pieces of information, such as a set of scores from a game.

If you have a variable or list on the stage, you can change its position by dragging.

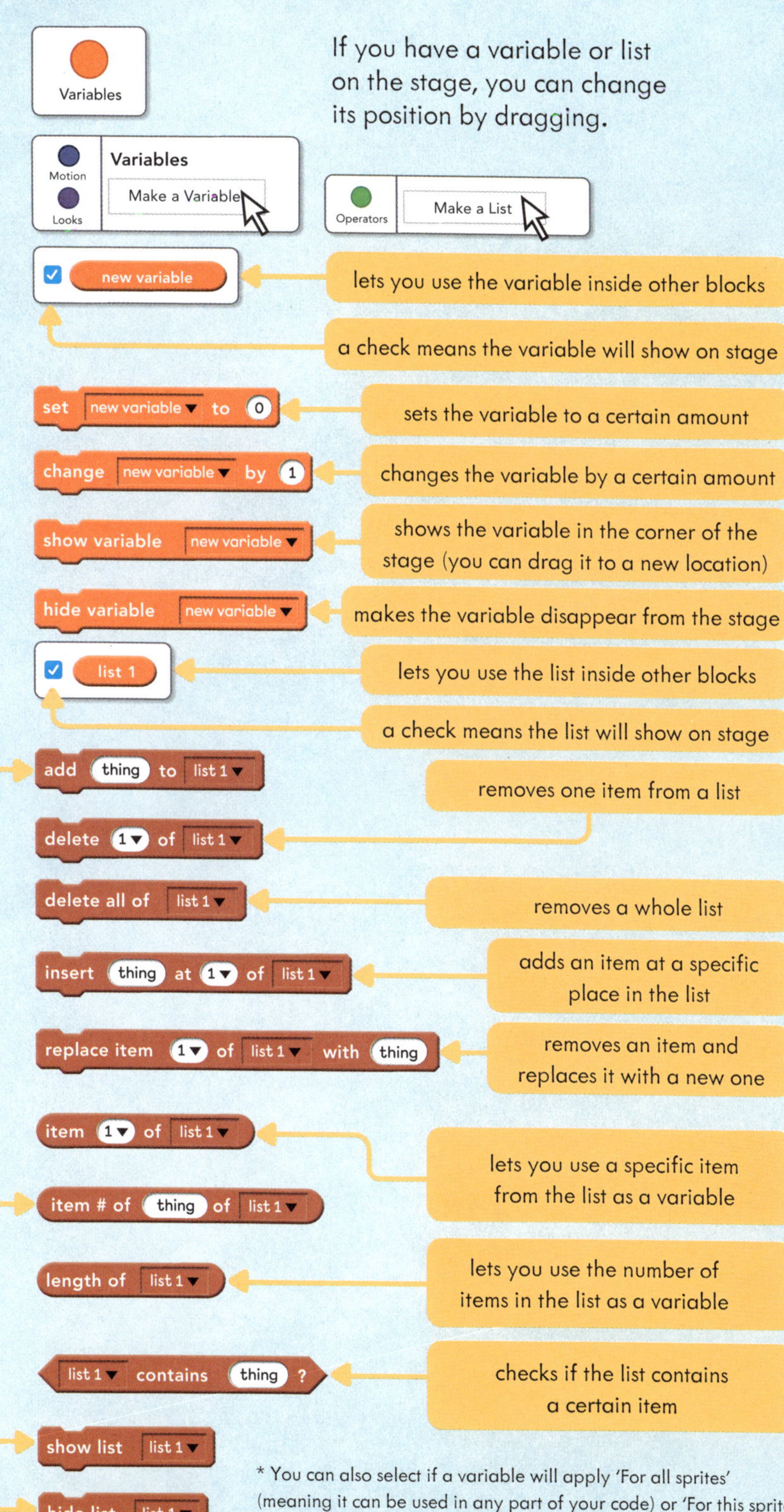

* You can also select if a variable will apply 'For all sprites' (meaning it can be used in any part of your code) or 'For this sprite only' (meaning it can only be used for that particular sprite).

MY BLOCKS

My Blocks allows you to make your own **custom** blocks, each containing a reusable section of code. This is something coders often do – in other computer languages, it's known as making a **routine.**

You click on 'Make a Block'...

give your new block a name (e.g. 'new block')...

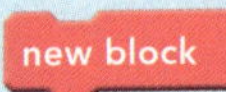

...and a **define** block will appear in the **script area.**

Add blocks underneath it to tell the computer what your new block should do.

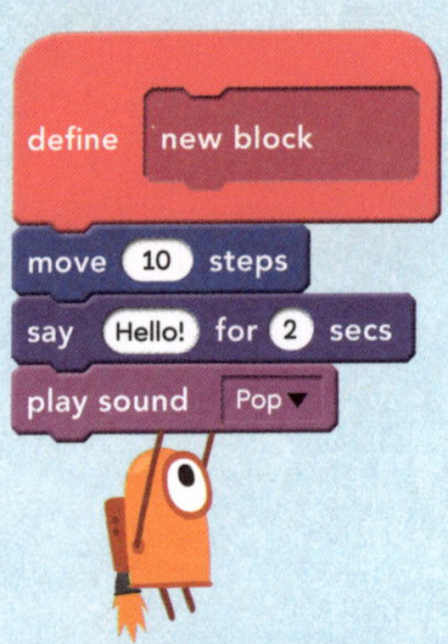

Your new block will then appear in the **My Blocks** menu. You can use it as a shortcut, so you don't have to build the same stack of blocks again and again; or you can use it to change the way those blocks run (see option 3 on the right).

New block options

When you're making a new block, you can choose to add different features.

1 Include a space to snap in other blocks, so you can add variables or conditions...

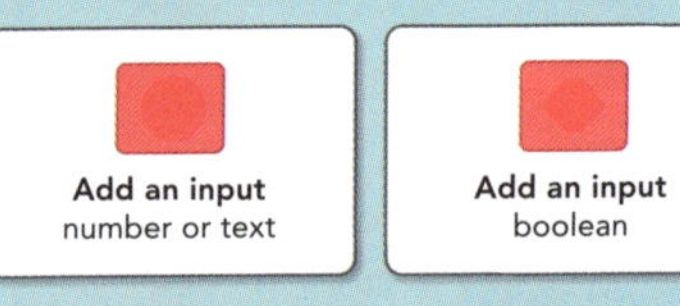

2 ... or include a label with information about the new block.

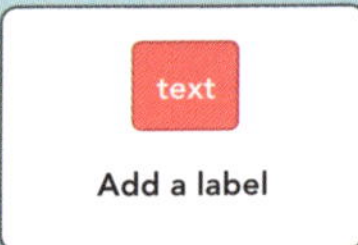

3 Check 'Run without screen refresh' to make the new block run without 'refreshing' or updating the picture on screen until everything it contains is finished.

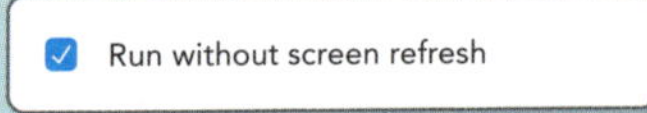

EXTENSIONS

Extensions contains extra menus and blocks, including **Pen** and **Music** blocks. Just click the **Extensions** button and select an option to make them appear.

PEN

Pen blocks allow you to draw using a sprite.

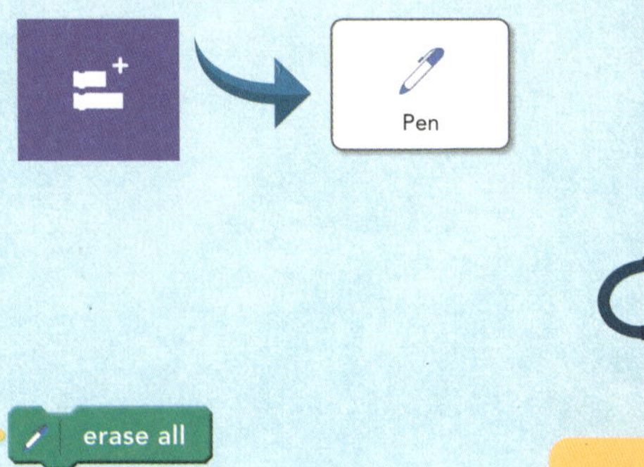

clears all pen drawings off the stage → erase all

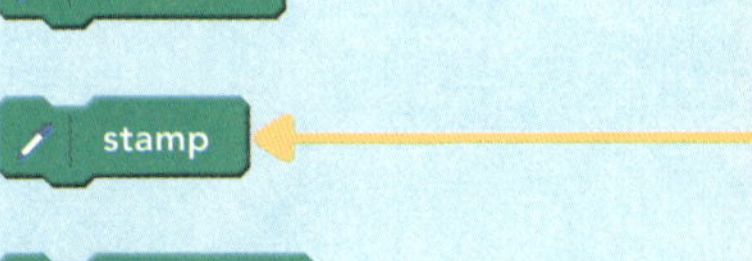

stamp ← 'stamps' an image of a sprite onto the stage (this is just an image, *not* a new sprite)

makes the sprite leave a pen trail as it moves → pen down

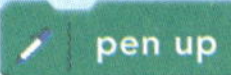

pen up ← makes the sprite stop leaving a pen trail

sets the color of the pen by clicking on the screen (the color where you click will become the pen color) → set pen color to

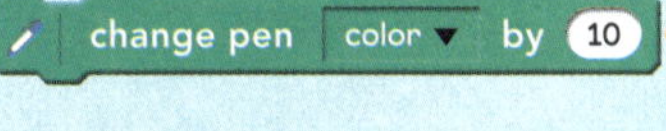

change pen color by 10 ← changes the color or effect (selected from the drop down menu) by a certain amount

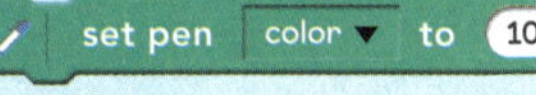

gives the pen a color or an effect (selected from the drop down menu) using the numbers → set pen color to 10

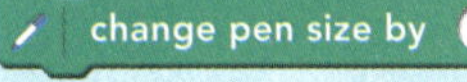

change pen size by 1 ← makes the pen bigger or smaller by a certain amount

sets the pen size → set pen size to 3

MUSIC

See page 84.

Glossary

animation A series of images shown one after another, to make it look as if things are moving.

backdrop In *Scratch*, the picture in the background of the *stage*.

Backdrop Library In *Scratch*, a list of available *backdrops*.

Backdrop button In *Scratch*, the button which opens the *Backdrop Library*.

Backpack Part of a *Scratch account* where you can store *sprites*, *backdrops* and *scripts* to use later.

binary A system of counting with 1s and 0s, used by all *computers*.

bitmap In computing, an image made up of individual dots of color or *pixels*. In *Scratch*, a *painting* mode which lets you draw pixel by pixel.

block In *Scratch*, a unit of *code* which can be put together with other blocks to make a *script*.

block menu In *Scratch*, a group of *blocks* of a particular kind, such as *Motion* (movement) or *Looks* (appearance).

Boolean block In *Scratch*, a *reporter block* with only two options: true/yes or false/no.

Boolean logic A way of working things out, used by all *computers*, which involves breaking decisions down into simple yes/no questions.

BPM Beats per minute, used to measure the *tempo* of music.

broadcasting In *Scratch*, sending a message from one part of the *code* to another.

bug An error in *code* which stops a *program* from running properly.

byte A unit used to measure amounts of *computer data*. See also *megabyte*.

C-block In *Scratch*, a *block* which wraps around other blocks to form a C-shape, such as *loops* and *if...* blocks. The shape helps to control *syntax* and make the structure clear.

cap block In *Scratch*, a *block* which finishes or 'caps' a *script*; these blocks can't have another block added below.

clear To wipe clean or *delete* something, usually from the screen.

click Selecting something by clicking the mouse button (always the *left* mouse button, unless it says 'right-click').

clone An identical copy. In *Scratch*, it means a copy of a *sprite*.

code Instructions written in *computer language*, telling a *computer* what to do.

coding Writing instructions for a *computer*.

computer A machine designed to follow instructions and process *data*; this is sometimes described as taking *input* and turning it into results or *output*.

computer language A language designed for *computers*, with a set word list and *syntax*; *Scratch* is one example.

computer logic The basic rules which all *computers* follow.

condition In computing, something which a *computer* must consider before making a decision. In *Scratch*, conditions are set by *Boolean blocks*.

conditionals Instructions which tell the *computer* to react differently to different conditions, such as 'if' or 'repeat until'.

constant In computing, a piece of *data* which is fixed (the opposite of a *variable*).

Control menu In *Scratch*, a group of *blocks* used to control other blocks or *scripts*.

coordinates A way of dividing an area into a grid and measuring distances, so you can find things by how far left/right (*x coordinate*) and up/down (*y coordinate*) they are.

costumes In *Scratch*, different versions of the same *sprite*.

cropping Trimming the edges of a picture.

cursor The flashing line which shows where your typing will appear on-screen. Also sometimes used as another name for the *mouse-pointer*.

custom block In *Scratch*, a single *block* which can contain a whole set of others. You can make your own custom blocks in the *My Blocks menu*.

data Information used by a *computer*. Any data that might change must be labeled – usually by creating *variables* or *lists*. A piece of data that does not change is sometimes described as a *constant*. See also, *string*.

debugging Fixing *code* to remove errors or *bugs*.

delete To remove something from the *computer's* memory.

double-click To click the left mouse button twice.

download To *save* something from a *website* onto a *computer*.

drag In computing, to move an item while holding down a mouse button. In racing, a force which slows things down.

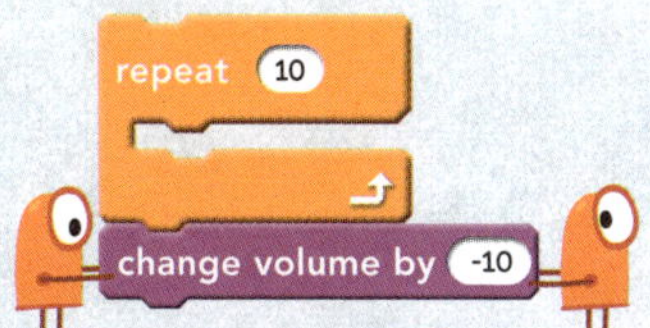

drop-down menu A list of options which appears when you *click*.

duplicate Create an identical copy.

ellipse A round or oval shape.

Events menu In *Scratch*, a group of *blocks* used for starting and stopping *scripts*.

Extensions In *Scratch*, extra *blocks* which can be added to the block menus.

file A set of information saved on a *computer*. Different types of files have different letters or *file extensions* at the end.

file extension The set of letters after the dot in a *file name*, which tells the *computer* what kind of information is in the *file*. For example .jpg is an image and .wav is a sound.

file name What you call a *file* when you *save* it on a *computer*.

flow chart A type of diagram which can be used to plan each step of a *program*.

folder A way of grouping together different *computer files* when you *save* them.

font A style of lettering.

graphic effects Effects which change the appearance of a picture.

green flag button In *Scratch*, starts all *scripts* with a 'when green flag clicked' *start block*.

hat blocks See *start blocks*.

icon In computing, a small picture which represents something, such as a *file* or a set of controls.

if/else In computing, a *conditional* instruction which tells the *computer* what to do in two situations.

if/then In computing, a *conditional* instruction which tells the *computer* what to do in one situation.

infinite scroller A type of game which carries on until the player makes a mistake.

input Information or instructions which you put into a *computer*.

internet A huge network which allows *computers* around the world to communicate with each other.

keywords Instruction words with a fixed, precise meaning for the *computer*, such as 'move' or 'play'.

layers A way of dividing pictures so that some parts appear in front of others.

level A challenge to complete in a *computer* game.

list A way of organizing any number of pieces of information for a *computer*.

logging in Accessing a *computer* account by entering a *username* and password.

Looks menu In *Scratch*, a group of *blocks* used to change how things appear on the *stage*.

loop A section of *code* which repeats.

megabyte Just over one million (1,048,576) *bytes*.

menu A list of options.

messaging In computing, sending information between different parts of a *program*; in *Scratch*, this is done by *broadcasting*.

Microphone In *Scratch*, an option in a pop-up menu that lets you record sounds.

Motion menu In *Scratch*, a group of *blocks* used to move *sprites* around the *stage*.

mouse-pointer The arrow you see on screen, which is controlled by moving the mouse.

Music extension In Scratch, a group of blocks which control music.

My Blocks menu In *Scratch*, a *block menu* which allows you to create your own *custom blocks*.

My Stuff If you have a *Scratch account*, this is where your projects will be saved.

nested loop A *loop* inside a loop.

offline When a *computer* is not connected to the *internet*.

online When a *computer* is connected to the *internet*.

Operators menu In *Scratch*, a group of *blocks* used for doing mathematics and setting out *conditions* with *Boolean logic*.

output The results you get from a *computer*.

paintbrush In *Scratch*, an option in a pop-up menu that brings up *painting tools*.

painting tools In *Scratch*, a set of tools which allow you to create your own *sprites* and *backdrops*.

palette In computing, a display of available options (usually colors).

Pen extension In *Scratch*, a group of *blocks* used for drawing with sprites.

pixelate A *graphic effect* which breaks up a picture into large colored dots.

pixels The colored dots which make up the picture on a screen.

program A set of instructions in *computer language*, which tells a *computer* what to do.

random Not decided by a pattern or system, so it's impossible to predict.

red button In *Scratch*, this stops all *scripts*.

remix In *Scratch*, a new version of a project, in which the *code* has been altered.

repeat forever In computing, an instruction which makes a section of *code* repeat endlessly. In *Scratch*, this is done by a *C-block*.

repeat until In computing, an instruction which makes a section of *code* repeat until a certain condition is met. In *Scratch*, this is done by a *C-block* with a *conditional*.

reporter block In *Scratch*, a *block* used inside another block, and which contains a value (such as a *variable* or a *string*) which it then 'reports' to the block around it.

right-click To click the right-hand mouse button.

rotation style In *Scratch*, the way a *sprite* turns around if it reaches the edge of the *stage*.

routine In computing, a named, reusable section of *code*; in *Scratch*, this is done by *custom blocks*.

run To set a *program* or *script* going.

save To store *computer files* so you can use them again later. With *Scratch*, you can do this *online* in your *Scratch account* or *offline* on your *computer*.

Scratch A *computer language* designed especially to teach beginners about *coding*.

Scratch account A way of using *Scratch online*, which allows you to store your projects and share them with others.

Scratcher A person who uses *Scratch*.

screen refresh When a *computer* updates the picture on screen.

script In *Scratch*, a set of instructions made by stacking *blocks* of *code* together.

script area In *Scratch*, the part of the screen where you stack up *blocks* of *code* into *scripts* for a selected *sprite*.

scroll Move around the visible part of the screen, usually by sliding a bar on the right and another at the bottom.

Sensing menu In *Scratch*, a group of *blocks* which make *sprites* react to certain *conditions*.

slider A button which enables you to move smoothly through a range of numbers.

Sound menu In *Scratch*, a group of *blocks* which control sound effects.

Sounds Library In *Scratch*, the sounds available to use.

speaker button In *Scratch*, the button which opens the *Sounds Library*.

special effects See *graphic effects*.

sprite In *Scratch*, a picture (of anything, including text) to which you can attach *scripts*.

sprite area In *Scratch*, the part of the screen where you can see all the *sprites* used in a project.

sprite button In *Scratch*, the button which opens the *Sprite Library*.

Sprite Library In *Scratch*, a list of the *sprites* available to use.

stack In *Scratch*, a set of *blocks* that have been joined together.

stack block In *Scratch*, an ordinary rectangular *block* which accepts other blocks above and below.

stage In *Scratch*, this is where you see your *code* run. It also has its own code area where you can attach *scripts* to control *backdrops* and background effects.

start blocks In *Scratch*, these activate all the *blocks* attached underneath them. Also called *hat blocks*.

start screen The first screen you see in a *computer* game, also known as a *title screen*.

string In computing, a sequence of letters or numbers that the computer treats as characters (that is, not as a number).

syntax A way of setting out *code* so a *computer* will be able to understand it.

tempo The speed of music, measured in *BPM*.

Text tool In *Scratch*, a *painting tool* which allows you to add letters to your picture.

title screen See *start screen*.

upload To send *data* or *files* from your *computer* to somewhere else, usually so the contents can be used or viewed *online*.

username A name you use to register for an online service, such as a *Scratch account*.

variable A way of labeling information for a *computer*, so it can keep track of items that might change.

Variables menu In *Scratch*, a group of *blocks* used to deal with *variables* and *lists*.

vector image In computing, an image made up of individual shapes. In *Scratch*, a painting mode which lets you draw with shapes.

webcam A camera connected to a *computer*.

website A page (or group of pages) which you can look at on the *internet*.

window In computing, a framed area of the screen displaying the information for one *program*.

x coordinate A number which decides how far left-right across a grid (in *Scratch*, the *stage*) something appears.

y coordinate A number which decides how far up-down on a grid (in *Scratch*, the *stage*) something appears.

zoom in Make a picture larger, so you can see more detail.

zoom out Make a picture smaller, so you can see more of it.

Index

Edited by Jane Chisholm
Additional illustrations by Matt Bromley
Additional designs by Tom Lalonde, Mike Olley and Samuel Gorham
Code tested by Laura Cowan, Matthew Oldham and Amy Chiu
Revised and updated by Jordan Akpojaro, with thanks to Victoria Williams

This revised edition first published in 2022 and updated in 2024 by Usborne Publishing Limited, 83-85 Saffron Hill, London EC1N 8RT, United Kingdom. usborne.com First published in America 2022 and updated in 2024. This edition published 2024.